First day of forever

First day of forever

And Other Stories
for LDS Youth

Jack WEYLAND

INTERNATIONAL STANDARD BOOK NUMBER
0-88290-136-2

LIBRARY OF CONGRESS CATALOG CARD NUMBER
80-82455

HORIZON PUBLISHERS CATALOG AND ORDER NUMBER
2037

Second Printing, January 1982

Printed and Distributed in the
United States of America
by

**Horizon
Publishers &
Distributors**

P.O. Box 490
50 South 500 West
Bountiful, Utah 84010

Foreword

I don't know when it started.

Maybe with my parents. As a boy, I remember hours spent with them in a car parked downtown, doing what they called "watching the people," looking at the endless parade of shoppers flowing past us. The way to avoid a spanking was to make up stories about the people shuffling by. To this day I still am watching.

Or maybe it started with being a reporter for a junior high school paper, or with the experience of working on a college literary magazine at Montana State University.

However it started, this is how it bore fruit. In the summer of 1971 my family and I were at BYU, where I was doing high pressure physics research. We stayed in off-campus housing. Since there was no lawn to mow or water, or garden to tend, no church callings to work on, I had time on my hands. I decided to take a BYU correspondence course in creative writing.

In the first lesson, I wrote my instructor and asked if I could write a few stories instead of completing the lesson material. He agreed to this. The first story was "You Can't Save Cotton Candy." Since the course cost $37.50, I decided to see if I could get my money back. I sent the story to *The New Era* Magazine. They accepted it, and sent me enough money to pay for the course.

After the summer ended, we returned to South Dakota. I decided to write one more story about the difficulties I had in getting a testimony. Within a month, *The New Era* had accepted my second story.

It seemed easy enough, but they rejected my third story, and I decided to quit writing. After all, someone trained in science shouldn't waste time making up stories.

I would have stopped were it not for Brian Kelly, editor of *The New Era*. He encouraged me to continue writing. In fact, he was so enthusiastic that I began to doubt his judgment—but I did continue to write.

Therefore, much of any tribute these stories may receive goes to Brother Kelly and his staff. I will always be grateful to them for their help and encouragement.

I express my appreciation to The Church of Jesus Christ of Latter-day Saints for giving permission to publish this collection which has appeared in *The New Era* over the past ten years.

Finally, my thanks to Horizon Publishers for being willing to take a chance on a book of short stories.

I love the youth of the Church. I realize I can't entirely understand their struggles into adulthood, but I remember mine and write about them, and hope that sometimes I hit a common chord between them and me.

Contents

First Day of Forever

After the temple vows were spoken, after the pictures of the bride and groom were taken outside on the snowy grounds of the Idaho Falls Temple, after Steve and Cathy changed into warm sweaters and ski slacks for their trip, after parting hugs and kisses with parents—finally they were alone, Mr. and Mrs. Steve Holland, driving north for a three-day honeymoon at his uncle's cabin in Montana.

"I'm a married lady!" she burst out suddenly a few miles out of Idaho Falls. "I'm somebody's wife!"

"You sure are," he smiled.

"I'm so happy! It's all come true—my greatest dream. Ever since I was a little girl, I've been praying that some day I'd be married in the temple. And it's come true."

She snuggled close to him. "Steve, when you were in high school, did you ever think about who you'd marry?"

"Sure. I remember I used to look through each month's issue of the *New Era*. I'd find a picture of a really neat-looking girl, and I'd think to myself, maybe she'll be my wife someday. And for that whole month I'd have her picture on my wall and I'd try to do the things she'd want me to do. I was true to her—until the next issue."

"You've never told me that before," she said.

He grinned and reached out to touch her cheek. "I guess there's still a few things we don't know about each other. I bet you don't even know what my favorite food is."

"Hamburger," she answered quickly.

"No."

"Steve, that's all you ever ate in your apartment at school."

"But it's not my favorite."

"Steak? Pizza? Spaghetti?"

"Sorry," he teased.

Suddenly she looked at him as if he were a total stranger. "You're kidding!"

"No. It's ham and lima beans."

"Oh," she said, moving away from him so she could take off her ski parka. She stayed on her side of the car.

They entered Rexburg. Steve drove around the Ricks College campus, savoring the bustling energy of students changing classes, and then drove back on to the highway north.

She didn't say much for a long time. Finally she asked, "Steve, are you even just a bit apprehensive?"

"Maybe I am—just a little."

"Me, too," she confessed, "just a little. When I saw those girls at Ricks, I realized that I've left that for good. I'll never be a coed again. I guess that sounds silly, doesn't it?"

It was several miles before she could ask him, "What are you apprehensive about?"

He reached for her hand. "Not about you, Cathy. I'm absolutely sure about my love for you."

She let out a small sigh and moved closer to him.

"It's just that I've been looking forward to that one big goal called temple marriage for so long and somehow I've never pictured what happens in a marriage a week after the ceremony, or a year, or a decade. Do you understand?"

"I think so," she said. "It's like those children's stories where the handsome prince carries the fair maiden away to his castle. The end. But what do the fair maiden and the handsome prince do for the next 60 years?"

"They live happily ever after," Steve said.

"We will, won't we?" she asked with sudden concern in her voice.

"I hope so, Cathy. I really hope so."

"Steve, you won't die early, will you? Promise me you won't."

"This is our wedding day. We're not supposed to think about death."

"What if we have a baby that dies or is born a cripple? Steve, I couldn't bear that. God won't let it happen, will he?"

He shook his head. "I don't know."

"All of a sudden," she said soberly, "marriage seems such a heavy responsibility."

They rode in silence for several miles.

Finally Steve tried to break the somber mood they were in. "We'll be at my uncle's cabin in about three hours. It'll be great! My uncle told me they went up last night to get it ready for us. They've got enough firewood split for four days, and they've filled the refrigerator with food."

"It sounds nice," she said quietly.

"Is anything wrong?" he asked her.

"There's one thing I need to ask you. Can we start even the first day of our marriage with family prayer at night?"

"I promise," he answered.

Then the spell was broken. She sat very close to him and asked meekly, "Tell me how to cook lima beans and ham."

They continued north, finally crossing the Idaho-Montana border.

"It looks like we might get a little snow," he said, understating his concern at the snow clouds in front of them.

Ten miles from a small town, the red alternator light flashed on. He thumped the glass to see if he could get it to turn off, but it stayed lit.

"It's probably nothing, but we'll have to stop at the next town and have somebody look at it."

By the time they reached the four-store town, the snow was coming down heavily. They pulled into the gas station and parked. They went in, and Steve explained the problem to the attendant, who agreed to look at it as soon as he finished another car.

Steve and Cathy waited in the office, walking around restlessly, idly reading the instructions on oil additives. The room smelled of stale cigars. A desk in the corner of the office was strewn with piles of paper.

Two men, laughing loudly, stumbled across the road from the bar and entered the station.

"Hank? Where are you?" one of them yelled, taking off his cowboy hat and revealing a nearly bald scalp.

"Hank? Come on, close up! Come with us over to Pete's Place. We'll buy you a drink," the other called. His stomach protruded well beyond the confines of his wide western belt.

They both walked into the garage part of the station. "You're not going to get much business tonight. There's a big storm coming. We heard it on the radio."

"Just one more job and I'll close it down," the mechanic replied.

"We'll wait." The one who was paunchy stayed in the garage, but the other sat down on the chair in front of the desk, propped his feet on the desk, and took a long drink from his can of beer.

"You folks going far?" he asked.

"Just to Big Sky," Steve answered.

"Glad it's not me traveling tonight. Big storm coming. You'd better stay here tonight. That other guy—his name is Oscar—he runs the Star Motel. Gives winter rates, too. Of course," he said with a wink, "maybe you're not married."

"We're married," Cathy said firmly. "We were married today."

"No kidding? Hey, Oscar," he yelled, "come here!"

The second man stepped into the office.

"Oscar, these good people just got hitched today. Now I told 'em that they ought to stay at your place instead of bucking the storm. How about it?"

"You bet! You can have my best room. The TV works, and I'll even throw in some free donuts and coffee in the morning."

"No," Steve answered firmly. "We'll be going on."

Oscar drifted back out to talk with the mechanic, but the other man sat down again and opened another can.

"You got a dog?" he finally asked Steve.

"No."

"Well, let me tell you something. You get yourself a dog before your wife gets too set in her ways."

"You like dogs?" he asked Cathy.

"They're okay."

"They're a lot better than okay," the man said. "A dog'll never let you down, never complains when you don't get home on time." Fumbling for his wallet, he pulled out a picture and handed it to Steve. "Ain't she something? She's real pretty, huh?"

"Yes," Steve answered.

"She's part German shepherd and part wolf. But you know what?" the man continued. "My wife hates that dog. It's her own fault, too."

He bent the empty can in two and tossed it into the already full wastepaper basket. He wiped his mouth and continued his story.

"My wife's got false teeth. When the dog was just a pup, my wife left the teeth on the kitchen table overnight. Well, you know how pups are when they're young. When we got up next morning, there were pieces of false teeth all over the place. That pup chewed up my wife's teeth! Ain't that something?" He reared back in his chair, laughing crazily.

The laughing brought Oscar from the garage; he added some other details about how long it took to get another set of false teeth and how his friend's wife wouldn't go out in public until they came. That started them both laughing again.

"You just got hitched, huh?" Oscar asked. "Well, it's too late to help you now, boy!" he joked. Placing his hand on Steve's shoulder, he said, "Let me give you a little advice. Lay the law down right at first. Because if you don't she's gonna run all over you."

"I told 'em he ought to get him a dog right off," the other man added.

"That's good advice, real good advice."

A few minutes later the mechanic was done with the other car. He had Steve pull his car into the vacant stall in the garage.

When he walked back into the office from the garage, he found that Cathy was outside, huddled by the door, her parka hood zipped up, tears in her eyes, staring out at the snow.

"You'll get cold out here," he said, putting his arm around her.

"I had to get away from there. To those men their wives are the enemy. What went wrong in their marriages?"

"It won't happen to us."

"Steve, it's only been six hours since we were in the temple, and now look where we are."

After a few minutes of work by the mechanic, they were back on the road.

The storm seemed much worse after leaving the security of the lights of the small town. The entire road was completely covered with snow so that it became difficult to judge where the center line was.

Steve leaned forward, his arms and back tense as he nervously concentrated on driving. Darting swirls of snow raced across the road.

A car suddenly jumped out of the swirling snow coming toward them. Steve tried to judge where the center line would be if he could see it.

The car was heading directly toward them. "Get over!" Steve yelled. He cranked the wheel hard to the right to avoid a collision, and the car breezed by, tossing up a giant cloud of snow into the air.

They were off the shoulder of the road. Steve gunned the engine, trying to power out of the slope, but the back wheels spun, causing the back end to slide farther down the slope. In order to correct for that, he steered the car farther down the incline. The snow brought them finally to an almost gentle stop.

He slammed his fist at the steering wheel in frustration. Turning to her, he asked, "You okay?"

"I'm all right."

He got out of the car and walked around it. The snow was above his knees. Opening the trunk of his car, he rummaged around until he found a small shovel that he used for camping.

He walked to the front of the car and began to furiously scoop up small mounds of snow.

Suddenly she was next to him. "Steve, stop. It's snowing faster than you can shovel."

"You shouldn't be out here."

"Look, I'm not some helpless glass doll that you have to handle carefully or I'll break. I'm your wife, and I go with you wherever you go—into the temple, or into run-down gas stations, and, if it happens, into snow banks."

"I should've listened to that man in the gas station. We should've stayed in his crummy motel. But no, I have to have my grandiose schemes. What a dumb thing. You married an idiot."

"We're both alive, the car's okay, so what's the big deal?"

He looked at her, surprised at her strength. "Yeah?"

"Yeah," she barked out in a fake gangster voice. "And another thing, quit knocking the man I married because I love him." She snuggled close and kissed him.

"Steve, I'm part of this marriage, too. I can help out."

"How can you help out now?" he asked, amused by the thought of her pulling the car out of the snow.

"By telling you that while you were putting on that impressive snow shoveling demonstration, I thought I saw a light through the trees back there."

"Oh," was all he said.

They started toward the light seen just faintly through the trees. It was a small house. There was a look of severity about the place, as if something had forced a style of life that was ordered but without joy.

They stood on the porch and knocked. "Cathy, if we can help it, let's not tell them we just got married. I can't stand any more free advice."

"You ought to get a dog," she mimicked.

A porch light flashed on, exposing them to unseen inspection. The door opened a crack. "What do you want?" a man's voice asked harshly.

"Our car went into the ditch. My wife and I need some help."

Seconds passed. "Martin, ask 'em in," a woman's voice chided.

A man opened the door, allowing them just enough room to enter. He was a giant of a man, his face roughened and carved by years of being outdoors.

"What do you want from us?" he asked suspiciously.

"If you have a tractor, could you pull us out?"

"I've got a tractor, but I'm not pulling you out tonight."

"Why not?" Steve asked.

"We just heard on the radio that they've pulled off the highway crews. They advise no travel."

"We've only got another 20 miles to go."

"Look. I'm not pulling you out just to have you go over the canyon ten miles from here."

"We've got to get to my uncle's place tonight," Steve said, feeling his temper mount. "So how do we get there?"

"You don't. Not tonight. You don't know this country like I do."

The woman, thin and plain and eroded by her fight against the sterile land, stepped out of the shadows of the dimly lit room.

"You're welcome to stay with us. Aren't they, Martin?"

"I don't see what else they can do," he mumbled.

"They could stay in David's room."

"No! They aren't staying there!" the man erupted. "It's his room!"

"Martin, it's been 15 years!" she complained.

"Don't get me mad, Ella. The answer is no!" He hurried to a coatrack and put on a heavy sheepskin coat. "I'm going to chop some more wood," he said, biting off the words.

Steve stole a quick glance at Cathy.

The woman walked to the door and looked at the footprints left by her husband. She turned around slowly, a strange heaviness in her eyes. As she saw Steve and Cathy standing in the middle of the room, she took on the role of hostess. "I'm sorry. Let me get your coats. Please sit down. I'm Mrs. Gibson."

They talked for several minutes about the weather. Finally Mrs. Gibson asked, "How long have you been married? My guess is less than a week."

They both grinned sheepishly. "Does it show that much?"

"When a girl twists her wedding ring like that, I think it means that she hasn't been wearing it long."

"We were married today in Idaho Falls," Steve said, taking hold of Cathy's hand.

"Look," she said, brightening up, "let me fix you a little snack in the kitchen and then we can talk. Would you like to play some records? They're old, but you might like some of them."

She picked up some old 78 rpm records from a shelf and placed them on a coffee table in front of Cathy and Steve. "These are records of Glenn Miller. Martin and I used to play them when we were first married. That was a long time ago, during the Second World War. By the way, do you like tuna fish?"

She went into her kitchen to work. Steve put a few of the records on the phonograph.

"Do you know where I met Martin?" she asked them, coming to the kitchen entrance to talk. "At the five and ten store in Missoula. I was only 18 then. He was home from the army on a 30-day leave. It was a couple of days before Valentine Day, and I was working at the jewelry counter. After about a half an hour, he finally picked out something. He thrust it into my hand, paid for it, and asked if I'd gift wrap it. Well I did, but when I gave it to him, he just looked down, shook his head, gave it back, and mumbled, 'It's for you.' And that was the beginning. Since he was going overseas in just a few weeks, we ended up getting married before he left."

They listened to the records while they ate their snack.

"When Martin came back from the war, he worked at various jobs for a few years, and then we got a chance to get this place. It had belonged to his father. We've been here ever since."

After the last record on the stack had played, she showed them the necklace. It was a tiny chain with a small silver heart in the middle. "I think it cost all of two dollars. Oh, there's an inscription on the back. Can you still read it?"

"It says, 'Love is forever.' " Cathy slowly read the worn inscription.

"I haven't thought about that necklace for years."

"I bet there are some grandchildren in your life," Cathy said with a smile.

"No," she said bleakly. "We had a son, David, but he was killed in Vietnam."

"Oh, I'm sorry," Cathy said quickly.

"It's been hardest on my husband. He needed to have grandchildren to show off the ranch to, but we're all alone now. He can't let go of the bitterness."

She took the necklace into the bedroom and then returned to the kitchen. Steve and Cathy played some more records.

Mr. Gibson stayed busy outside until supper.

They had homemade soup and biscuits. Mr. Gibson hunched over his bowl and ate without much talking.

"Martin," the woman said, uncomfortable with his silence, "they were just married today in Idaho Falls."

He looked up briefly. "Are you from Idaho?"

"No, I'm from Montana and Cathy is from Nebraska."

"Then why get married in Idaho?" he asked.

"We're both members of the Mormon church. We were married in the Idaho Falls Temple."

"Why there?"

Cathy tried to explain. "We believe that a wedding performed in a temple of our church can continue even after death. We wanted our marriage to last forever."

The man sat up and glowered at her. "Nothing lasts forever. You'll learn that soon enough, I reckon."

"I've never been more certain of what I'm saying," Cathy replied with a quiet firmness in her voice.

"Then you're a fool!" the man said abruptly.

"Martin, that's no way to talk to company," the woman complained.

"Who invited 'em? I didn't"

"Martin!"

"What do they know about life? They're just a couple of kids."

"Please excuse him; he's not used to company," the woman said.

Mr. Gibson got up from his chair and walked over to Steve and Cathy. "You two come with me, and I'll show you what life does to people and their ideas about forever."

They followed him into a small back bedroom. The blinds were pulled, and there was only one bare bulb hanging from the ceiling. The room was filled with pictures and trophys and sports equipment.

"Go ahead, look around."

As they examined each picture, it was as if they were viewing the growth of a small boy into a young man—pictures of a three-year-old being held on a quarter horse by his proud father, a seven-year-old standing beside his father displaying a string of fish, a thirteen-year-old wearing a 4-H jacket and showing a hereford steer he had raised, a boy kneeling beside a trophy elk he had shot, a seventeen-year-old beside a cute girl in a formal gown, a proud graduate in a black cap and gown, a nineteen-year-old in front of the small white house wearing an army uniform.

The last picture frame contained a telegram announcing the boy's death in combat in Vietnam.

"It took us 19 years to raise him," the man said bleakly, "but they killed him in one second with a land mine."

"We're both sorry," Cathy said.

"I don't need your sympathy," the man said bitterly. He reached down and picked up a fishing reel in his hand, turning it over slowly, studying it. "He was a good boy, and if he'd lived, by now he'd be married and have children, and I'd have some grandchildren, and life would have some meaning."

He put the reel down on the shelf and turned to confront them. "Who remembers my boy anymore?"

They didn't know what to say.

"Nobody does. Not anymore. This is all that's left of him. What you see in this room. A few pictures and some ribbons from a county fair. And when my wife and I die, somebody will buy the house and toss it all away."

He took a step toward them, his face in agony. "Now you tell me, where is this *forever* you keep harping about? Where is *forever* for my boy?"

Cathy threw her arms around him as if he were her grandfather. Steve could hear her crying. At first the man stood there mutely, his arms at his side, untouchable in his grief. But then, seeing that she shared his sorrow, he put an arm around her to comfort her.

A moment later she stepped back and said, "God loves your son. His body is destroyed but his spirit is alive. Someday his body and his spirit will come back together, and he will stand on this earth with a perfect body. I know that is true."

He examined her face, searching for any insincerity, but he found none.

She continued, "God has commanded that temples be built so that we can help those who have died to receive the rich blessings they might have had if they'd lived. Your boy will live again."

Somehow the despair that had filled the room lifted. Steve felt the sweet influence of the Holy Ghost bear witness to Cathy's words.

The man looked at her upturned face for a long time and then simply said, "Nobody's ever told me that before."

"Mr. Gibson," Cathy said, "today I was in one of those temples. I've never been more certain that God loves all his children. He loves your son David."

The man slowly nodded his head. "David was a good boy." Then looking around and seeing for the first time that it was only a room, he said simply, "It's cold in here, isn't it? Let's go in the living room and talk some more."

Steve, with his mission experience, began to teach Mr. and Mrs. Gibson the gospel.

At 10:00 Mrs. Gibson invited them into the kitchen for a piece of cake she'd baked especially for Steve and Cathy. While they were eating, the electric power went out. They lit a candle and finished.

"Martin, It's going to get cold tonight without our electric heater."

"We can all stay by the fire and keep warm," he said.

Huddled around the fire, with the wind howling outside, they continued to talk. At 2:00 A.M., Mrs. Gibson turned to her husband and asked, "Martin, what do you think?"

"It's the first thing I've heard that makes any sense. We better learn more about it, though, before we join."

Cathy burst out excitedly, "You and your wife and your son can be sealed together as a family forever! Steve and I want to go with you through the temple when you go!"

Mr. Gibson cleared his throat nervously and reached a little awkwardly for his wife's hand. "Ella and me have been through a lot together. It'd be nice to be together forever."

Finally they agreed that it was time for sleep. While Mr. and Mrs. Gibson went to get some blankets, Steve reached over and kissed Cathy. "You are a terrific missionary."

"Wasn't it special?" she asked happily. "I wouldn't have traded it for anything."

They sat and watched the fire. The embers that had been in the fire the longest glowed the deepest red.

"Cathy, are you still afraid of the future? We can't guarantee that we won't have the same unhappiness in our lives that they've had."

"I know," she said quietly.

"If you knew now that I'd die in a few years, or that a baby would suffer sickness, would you walk away from our marriage?"

"I used to think that Heavenly Father would spare me that kind of trial," she said.

"And now what do you think?"

"I think that a testimony of the gospel of Jesus Christ can help us live through whatever comes."

"You're not scared anymore?"

She shook her head thoughtfully. "Not anymore."

Mr. and Mrs. Gibson returned to the fire, carrying some blankets. They pulled the couch and two chairs close to the fireplace. Mr. Gibson piled two large logs on the fire. Then he placed a small gift in Cathy's hand. It was wrapped in tissue paper.

All he said was, "Don't open it until you're on your way tomorrow."

A few minutes later Cathy whispered something to Steve. He nodded his head and then spoke to Mr. Gibson. "I promised my wife something about tonight. Would it be all right if we had family prayer?"

By the next morning the storm had let up, and by 11:00 they had managed to pull the car back on the highway. Shortly after that, Steve and Cathy were on their way.

Not until they were unloading their suitcases from the car into the cabin did Cathy remember the small package on the back seat. Unwrapping it, she found the old necklace with the words inscribed on the back—"Love is forever."

The Award

Football season was over, but the glory lingered on. The high school team had enjoyed an undefeated season, romping over each opponent by at least two touchdowns.

Even after the season ended, the team stuck together. Some of them ate lunch on the balcony that overlooked the main dining area of the school cafeteria. Originally the tables on the balcony had been used by teachers so they could eat and still keep an eye on the students, but with a new addition to the building, the teachers moved into a faculty lounge, and the tables became available. There was no official reservation for the team to sit there, but it was just something understood by other students.

Kevin, a sophomore, was the only Mormon on the team. He wasn't as mean as some of the others, but he was faster. He played end and had caught eight touchdown passes during the season.

It had taken the team a while before they could accept him. After the season was over, they couldn't understand why he wouldn't drink with them on weekends. To make matters worse, he was the only one who worried about grades.

One day in January, as Kevin set his food tray on the table, the quarterback, Craig Williams, stood looking at the students eating lunch in the main dining area below them.

"Why are there so many ugly girls?" Craig asked.

"Look who's talking," someone shot back. "You've got a face like a Halloween mask."

"Well, that's different," Craig said with a grin, "I've got character and style. Besides, guys don't have to be goodlooking, but girls are supposed to."

Kevin sat down and ate his lunch.

"Now you take that girl, for instance," Craig continued. "I bet she's the ugliest girl in school."

The fullback, who loved competition, rose to the challenge. "You're crazy. I see one who's twice as bad as yours."

The competition continued as Kevin ate. Five of the team stood by the railing and bantered back and forth over their choices for the ugliest girl.

Finally they decided on one girl.

"If ugly were money, she'd be a millionaire," one of them said with a grin.

"She's easily the world champion," Craig agreed. "She deserves a trophy or something."

"How about a sweater with no opening for her neck so it'd hide her face?" someone joked.

"No," Craig laughed, "but why not give her an award? Maybe a corsage with a card telling her what we think about her. We could leave it taped on the outside of her locker. It'd be anonymous."

They all agreed it would be the perfect thing to do.

"Kevin, you're a scholar. Write us a poem for the award."

"What kind of poem?" he asked, finishing his custard pudding.

"A poem telling her how ugly she is," Craig answered.

Kevin took a napkin from his tray and began to work on a rhyme. He enjoyed the feeling of being part of the group. In a few minutes he finished and read aloud.

> "When we speak of ugly, you're
>   the subject of talk.
> You've got a face that could stop
>   a clock.
> Accept this gift for what it's worth;
> We think you're the ugliest girl
>   on earth."

They broke up into spasms of laughter.

"All right!" Craig shouted, still laughing.

"It's perfect! Let's all chip in some money, and I'll get a corsage on Saturday. We'll give it to her Monday."

"Who's going to give it to her?" someone asked.

"Does anybody know who she is or where her locker is?" Craig asked.

Kevin stood up to see who they were talking about. The girl sat alone, eating quickly, with her head lowered. He recognized her. She had a locker next to Colleen, an LDS girl he was dating.

"I do," Kevin said.

"Okay, you can deliver it. I'll get the corsage to you Monday in history class. You put your poem with it and tape it to the outside of her locker just before the bell rings."

After school Kevin drove Colleen home. She was one of five other LDS students in the high school.

When they got to her home, she invited him in for some cookies and milk.

"What's the name of the girl who has a locker next to yours?" he asked between bites of a chocolate-chip cookie.

"That's Mary Beth Allen. Why?"

"She's really awful, isn't she?"

"Is she? Do you know her?"

"No, I've just seen her around. She's ugly, though, that's for sure."

"She's not so bad when you get to know her."

"Who'd want to do that?" he joked.

"I don't know. If she'd just do something with her hair, she'd have more friends."

"Don't tell anybody," Kevin said, "but the guys on the team have chosen her the ugliest girl in school. We're giving her a corsage and a special poem I wrote."

He recited the poem to Colleen. When he finished, she looked at him in shock.

"You're not really going through with this, are you?"

"Sure, why not?"

"Do you know how that's going to make her feel?"

"I don't care how she feels."

"Kevin, you're the only member of the Church on the team. Doesn't that mean anything to you?"

"It's taken me all this time for them to accept me as part of the group. I'm not going to preach to them and destroy everything."

"But you're willing to destroy that girl, aren't you?" she asked.

"She's ugly. Even you agree to that," he shot back.

"She's a child of God."

"Okay, but she's an ugly child of God."

"I can see ugliness, but it's not in her. It's in you and your vigilantes!"

"What right have you got to be my conscience?" he asked.

"I'm not your conscience. If you feel guilty, that is your conscience."

"No girl is going to tell me what to do!" He got out of his chair, full of anger.

Before he left, he remembered they had a date. "Oh, what about tonight?" he asked.

"Forget it!" she said.

He spent a dateless weekend.

On Sunday during priesthood meeting, he made sure to volunteer to bless the sacrament in Sunday School, mainly to spite Colleen so she'd know that he didn't feel guilty about the award.

Before the sacrament song, the Sunday School president got up. "We should all be thinking about the Savior during this time. These young men who bless and pass the sacrament stand in the place of the Savior in this sacred ordinance. Let's see if we can't all be a little more reverent today."

After he finished breaking the bread, near the end of the sacrament song, he looked over the congregation to find where Colleen was sitting.

Finally he found her, in the back row with Mary Beth Allen sitting next to her.

"Why is she here?" he thought. "She's not a Mormon. She's not supposed to be here. Colleen must have invited her to get back at me."

He felt his face turning red and perspiration breaking out all over. His vocal cords tightened up, and he started to cough. He was sure he couldn't get through the prayer.

"Will you give the prayer on the bread?" he gasped to the other priest, who nodded his head.

The prayer was given, and the deacons lined up to receive the trays.

The room became quiet as the sacrament was passed.

Kevin sat down and leaned forward so he couldn't be seen by the congregation. His eyes fastened on the sacrament prayer he was to give, and it was as if he were reading it for the first time in his life.

"What would the Savior do about Mary Beth Allen?" he thought.

Once the question was asked, the answer was obvious.

By the time he was to offer the prayer on the water, he'd made up his mind. He would have no part in humiliating Mary Beth. He'd tear up the poem.

During Sunday School class, Colleen introduced Mary Beth. "Mary Beth and I have lockers next to each other, but we never really knew each other very well until yesterday when I phoned her. I asked her to come today because she's such a good person. I found out that she works with handicapped children every day for a couple of hours as part of her Christian service."

"That's wonderful," the teacher enthusiastically said.

"Oh, they're such special children," Mary Beth said, "I love them all."

After Sunday School and lunch, Kevin drove to Colleen's house. She let him in, and they talked about everything else but Mary Beth, until finally he pulled out a white handkerchief and waved it.

"I surrender!" he said with a grin. "I'll make sure we don't give her the award."

"Oh, but I want you to give her an award. You've already bought the corsage. No use wasting it."

"Girls," he muttered. "I'll never understand them."

"All we need to do is to change the message on the card. I've already written it." She handed him a small card:

"A group of athletes want you to know that we think you're a special person. Thanks for giving of yourself to work with handicapped children. You set a good example for all of us. We have chosen you the winner of our Extra-Mile Award."

"Well?" she asked.

"It's not exactly what the team had in mind. They'll kill me if they find out."

"You can handle them."

"Are you kidding? They're animals."

"I have faith in you."

On Monday, a little before lunch, Kevin received the corsage from Craig. He hurried to her locker before classes let out and taped the corsage box and the card onto it.

"Well, that's over," he thought, happy to get rid of the whole business.

"Did you give her the award?" Craig asked at lunch.

"Yes," Kevin answered without explaining any details.

On Tuesday, during announcements on the PA system, the principal gave the usual list of upcoming events and then, in addition, said, "A girl has asked me to thank the anonymous group of guys who gave her a corsage. She wants them to know that it means a great deal to her."

Kevin knew he was in trouble.

The team was waiting for him at lunch.

"All right, what'd you do?"

"I didn't use the poem. I used a different message."

They stood menacingly around him.

"What kind of message?"

"I told her she was special."

"I knew we never should've let a Mormon do it," the fullback complained.

"Special? Are you kidding? What's special about her?"

She works with handicapped children every day without getting paid."

"Why would she do a dumb thing like that?"

"I don't know," Kevin said. "She says she loves them."

Just then, Mr. Graham, the principal, climbed up the stairs toward them. They all felt threatened by him.

"Hey, Mr. Graham, how's it going?" one of them said sheepishly.

"I'm trying to find the group who gave Mary Beth Allen a corsage."

"Why?" Craig asked warily. "There wasn't anything wrong with the corsage, was there? You know, like a tarantula hiding in it?"

"No, but her mother called and asked me to thank them personally if I could find them."

"Oh," Craig said quietly.

"You see, Mary Beth has a kidney malfunction. In order to stay alive, she has to go on a dialysis machine periodically. Sometimes she gets discouraged. The award was the nicest thing that's happened to her for quite some time."

"You mean she's going to die?" someone asked.

"No, but she's had to face the possibility of an early death. It's been difficult for her."

"Then why does she work with children?" Craig blurted out.

"How do you know she works with children?" Mr. Graham asked.

That was the first time any of them could remember Mr. Graham smiling at them.

"I won't embarrass you by asking if you were the ones who gave her the award, but I want you to know there's a very grateful mother in this city."

Mr. Graham left them with their thoughts.

"Where is she?" Craig suddenly asked.

They leaned over the balcony and looked. In a few seconds they found her, sitting alone as usual, but this time wearing a corsage, even though it was now beginning to fade.

They stared in silence at the corsage.

"I'm going down to eat with her," Craig said, grabbing his tray and heading down the stairs.

"He's crazy," the fullback said. "What if someone sees him with her?"

The next day Craig ate lunch with the team.

"Well, how is she?" one of them asked.

"She's okay when you get to know her. I promised her a favor, and I'll need you guys to help me."

"What kind of favor?"

"I promised her that we'd show up in our football gear at the school where those handicapped children go. Some of the kids are real football fans. They'd be really happy if we visited them."

"I'm not going," one of the players said. "I don't want any kids climbing all over me."

"If they do, play with them. C'mon you guys, help me out."

They visited the school for handicapped children on Friday. When Mary Beth was with the children, she became a different person, radiating love and enthusiasm. The team helped the boys in the school put on the helmets and shoulder pads and taught them how to throw a football.

On Monday they met at lunch as usual. As Kevin approached the table with his tray, Craig leaned against the railing, looking down at the students below.

Finally he turned to face Kevin. "You know, it's strange."

"What is?"

"Well, we pick the person in school who everybody agrees is a loser, but then she turns out to be okay once we get to know her."

"So?" someone asked.

"Okay, maybe it's just a coincidence, but I've been thinking. What if it isn't?" Craig turned to view the crowded cafeteria. "What if every one of them turns out to be special in some way?"

"They're all children of God," Kevin finally dared to say.

The fullback swore and then said, "You guys are crazy! Life's very simple. There are winners, and there are losers. We're the winners, and the girls we date are the winners. The rest are all losers."

"But what if the things that make them winners aren't so easy to spot?"

The fullback shook his head, muttered something, and left. Several others followed him.

Craig and Kevin and a few others leaned over the railing and looked down at the other students again. There were so many of them—guys and girls in a variety of clothes and hair styles and shapes and nationalities, yet each one somehow important.

Finally Craig said quietly, "Let's give the award once a month."

Last of the Big-Time Spenders

Four months after his mission, Kevin Jensen had earned enough money to barely get him through one semester at State College, provided that he room in the basement of his 63-year-old aunt's home and that he work part-time in the morning as a custodian at the college. There was no money for non-essential items, and with his younger brother now ready to go on his mission, there was no hope for financial assistance from his parents.

On a cold January morning, he left his family, got on a bus, and shivered the 300 miles to the college town. His aunt, who didn't drive a car, had talked a neighbor lady into driving her to the depot to pick him up.

The next day was Sunday. Kevin walked his aunt to church and found himself being introduced to other retired and widowed friends of his aunt, while the Young Adults seemed to be always on the other side of the chapel.

The chorister for Sunday School was a girl his age with a smile that lit up the room, at least for Kevin. Although a common complaint of choristers is that people never look up from the hymnbooks, on that day Kevin didn't look at the book at all but happily kept his attention on the chorister. Referring to the Sunday School bulletin, he found that her name was Jenny Wells.

On Monday, Kevin registered for classes. Afterwards he went to the college bookstore to buy books. One look at the prices and he decided to check them out of the library.

While in the bookstore, he saw Jenny buying some books. He waited until she got in the long checkout line and then stepped in behind her.

31

He was still rehearsing in his mind how to start a conversation when she dropped one of her books. He bent over to pick it up for her. Unfortunately she bent over at the same time and they bumped foreheads.

"Sorry," he apologized. "You stay there and I'll get it." He bent over and picked it up for her.

"Are you all right?" he asked.

"Yes, thank you."

"This sounds corny, but I think we're going to be good friends."

"Are we? she smiled. "Why?"

"Because we're both LDS, and we're both going to college here."

"You're LDS? Have you been to church before?"

"Yesterday. I didn't get to the Young Adult class because the bishop wanted to talk to me. I just got back from my mission."

"Oh," she smiled, "that is interesting."

He walked her home to the dorm. Their breath made little puffs of clouds as they walked.

"Do you like to walk?" he asked.

"Yes, why"

"In a minute I'm going to ask you out. If you say, yes, you should understand that I don't have a car, so we'll be walking where-ever we go."

"I definitely like to walk."

"Good. There's one other thing. Money is a little tight now, but I've budgeted a dollar a week for dating. This means I can either go out once a month and spend four dollars, or go out once a week and spend one dollar. So you need to decide if you want the four-dollar date or the one-dollar date."

They stopped on a small bridge to look at the icy patterns made by a small stream that meandered through the campus. He turned to look at her, and for a second their eyes met, and he felt they both were communicating much more with their eyes than either of them would dare vocally.

"You're nice to look at," he said softly.

"Funny, I was thinking the same thing about you," she said.

A little embarrassed, they continued walking again.

"One other thing," he continued. "I can't buy you a hamburger after our date, so eat a big supper before we go out."

"Do you want me to eat my vegetables, too?" she teased.

"Whatever you've been eating in the past will be fine. It's done wonders."

"Are you ever going to actually ask me out?" she laughed.

"Okay, will you go out with me?"

"Yes."

"Do you want the four-dollar date or the one-dollar date?"

"The one-dollar date."

"For the one-dollar date we can go to the art exhibit on campus, or we can go to a seminar on aging, or we can watch the swim team practice, or we can go to the library and read old issues of *Life* magazine. If you want more action, we can go to the last hour of a dance at the student union building."

"The last hour?"

"After they quit taking tickets. It's up to you. The world is at your feet, all for a dollar."

"I'll take the art exhibit and the dance."

"An excellent choice."

Although they were joking, he found himself more enchanted by her each moment. He thought about just stopping and telling her that he was falling in love, but he was afraid to do that. Besides, the joking was fun.

"Afterwards we can stay on campus and buy a cup of hot chocolate for a quarter a cup, or we can pick up an entire box of hot chocolate mix for 89 cents and go back and mix up two cups in the lobby of your dorm. Your choice?"

"Have you ever worked for Burger King?"

"No, why?"

"I keep expecting you to break into singing, 'Have it Your Way.'"

It was snowing on Friday night as he walked to her dorm. When she came out of her apartment, he was again taken back by her beauty.

"I'm ready," she said breezily. "I ate a good supper, I ate all my carrots like a good girl, and I've got warm clothes." She stopped as she saw he wasn't smiling. "Is anything wrong?"

"You're such a classy lady. You deserve better than this."

"Feeling sorry for yourself because you're not rich?"

"If I just had a car and a little more money."

"I like you fine the way you are."

As he helped her on with her coat, she noticed the clipboard he had brought with him.

"What's that?"

"It's a clipboard."

"I know that!" she laughed. "But why did you bring it?"

Suddenly the fun was back with them again. "You don't know about clipboards?" he asked.

"What's there to know?"

"You'll see," he grinned.

They walked to the art show on campus. It was the first night of the exhibit. Hanging up their coats in the lobby, they entered the exhibit hall and stood in front of the first painting.

"I like the overall balance in the picture, don't you?" Kevin said, with an official ring to his voice.

"Yes."

Kevin made a point of writing something on his clipboard. Up and down the exhibit, people respectfully observed them, believing they were the judges for the exhibit.

Kevin stepped back, his hand touching his chin. "Notice how the brush strokes create a definite lifting effect."

Jenny was blushing a crimson red. A few people came closer to hear what Kevin was saying.

They walked to the next painting, called "Bird in Flight." It looked as if someone had put paint on tricycle wheels and ridden over the canvas. There was nothing to indicate a bird, or flight, and the entire canvas was one blotch of yellow, red, and blue.

Kevin assumed the art judge pose, hand stroking his chin, and said finally. "Oh, yes, I see the bird, don't you?"

By this time there were six people directly in back of them, straining to see a bird in the blotches.

Kevin stepped to the canvas and began to randomly assign separate sections of the canvas to parts of the bird, saying with great authority, "This, of course, is the beak, and this is the left wing, and this is a tree, and this is a lake, and this is the right wing."

None of it, of course, made any sense, but people began to whisper, "Oh, yes, I see."

Jenny's face was bright red, and she fought to avoid breaking down with laughter. With some difficulty, she whispered, "May I have a word with you privately?"

They walked quickly out of the exhibit area and up one flight of stairs. There they broke down with peals of laughter.

Finally she gasped, "They think we're art judges."

"Why should they think that?" I don't know anything about art."

"It's your clipboard, isn't it?"

"Yes, the magic of a clipboard."

"That was so funny."

"I'm glad you enjoyed it."

"But is it the right thing to do?"

"I don't know. We never said we were art judges."

"No, that's true."

"And if somebody came up and asked us if we were, we'd tell them no."

"Still," she said, "we're LDS, and we need to set a good example. Maybe we should go back there without the clipboard."

"Whatever you say."

They left the clipboard with their coats and returned. As they passed "Bird in Flight," someone who had watched Kevin was now pointing out enthusiastically to others the various parts of the bird.

At 11:00 they walked to the dance. As Kevin had predicted, the people taking money had long ago shut down. They danced until midnight, then walked to a small store that stayed open all night, bought some hot chocolate mix, and returned to her dorm.

At 1:00 he got up to leave.

"Jenny, thanks. You've been a good sport."

"I've enjoyed it."

"The only expense was for the box of hot chocolate mix."

"Oh, I'll get it for you," she said. "You can take it home."

"How about if I left it here and we used it on another date."

"That'd be fine."

"Would you like the three-dollar-eleven-cent date? That's how much is left for the month."

"A certain young man," Jenny began, sounding like a teacher, "can spend four dollars a month on dating. He can go out twice a month and spend two dollars a date, or four times a month at one dollar. How many times can he go out with the same girl at fifty cents a date?"

"Eight," Kevin answered.

"At a quarter a date?"

"Sixteen."

Jenny stopped and smiled. "I've never enjoyed mathematics so much."

Kevin left the dorm and started to walk home, still in a trance. He went over in his mind the way she was, and the excitement and fun he felt just being with her, and the way they had looked at each other a few times during the evening.

"Hey, Kevin, is that you?"

Kevin looked over to the car that had pulled over to the curb. It was Harly Mitchell, a former missionary companion.

"Want a ride, elder?"

Kevin got in the car. "Harly, I didn't know you were here!"

"One more year."

"Do you still go to church? I was there Sunday and didn't see you."

"We were visiting my in-laws. Showing off our baby."

Harly enthusiastically told Kevin about his wife and baby and what a financial struggle it was to stay in school. He was just then returning from a night job at a gas station.

"And what about you?" Harly asked. "Why are you up so late, elder?"

Kevin told him about Jenny.

"Do I hear wedding bells ringing?" Harly teased.

"No, we just like each other. Besides, I'm not going to get married until I'm out of school."

"Famous last words."

"I can't afford to be married."

"Who can? Say, why don't you bring Jenny over to our place for dinner next week? It'd give us a chance to talk some more."

Kevin accepted the invitation, but because of previous commitments to home teach on Harly's night off from the gas station, he had to schedule it for two weeks later.

On Wednesday of the next week, Kevin phoned and asked Jenny to go with him to a movie.

"Can you afford it?" she asked.

"Don't worry. I'm a big spender."

On Friday, the auditorium in the Agriculture Building was still only half filled as Kevin and Jenny sat down.

"Our first film tonight," a man in a western suit shyly announced, "will be 'Your Modern Poultry Industry.'" Kevin pulled out a large bag of homemade popcorn and shared it with Jenny.

"I'll never look at a chicken in the same way," Jenny joked as they left the auditorium after the movie.

Later they went to a dance for the last hour. Once after a song was over, while they still faced each other, he reached over and took hold of both her hands. Their eyes met and he felt himself wondering how he could stand to ever be apart from her again. He felt a sensation as he looked into her eyes of being allowed into a place in her heart she'd never let anyone else enter.

Fighting his feelings, he broke the spell by turning away and making a joke about the band.

"Are we going to talk about it?" Jenny asked quiety.

"About what?" Kevin asked nonchalantly.

"About what's happening to us?"

"What's happening to us? We're just learning about chickens."

She started to cry.

They stood on the edge of the dance floor, watching others dance. And then the dance was over, and they were alone except for those in the band carrying away their instruments.

"Why won't you talk about it?" she finally asked.

"I've got three more years of school, Jenny. You know that, don't you?"

She nodded her head.

On Saturday he took her to visit her aunt. They helped make bread. When it was finished, they sliced a loaf and had the warm bread with butter and honey and a glass of milk.

Sunday after sacrament meeting they went to a Young Adult fireside.

"I talked to my parents on the phone today. They'd like to meet you."

"Oh." He felt himself tense up.

"They like to meet all my friends," she quickly added. "They'll be in town Wednesday, and they've invited us out to dinner."

"What does your father do for a living?" Kevin asked.

"He works in a bank."

"Teller?"

"Vice-president."

They ate with her parents, who were not members of the Church, at the most expensive restaurant in town. At the end of the meal, they sat and talked.

"This isn't too bad a place, is it?" Jenny's mother said. "I think it was all rather decent food, don't you?"

"Actually, Jenny and I have been here before."

"Oh, what did you have?"

"Nothing," Kevin answered. "See that sign on the wall that says, 'Ask to visit our kitchen'? Well, that's what we did."

"With a clipboard," Jenny said with a smile.

"But surely you must have had something."

"Kevin's on a very tight budget," Jenny added quickly.

"Oh."

Kevin was angry at the way he felt. On one hand, he wanted to impress her parents. But he resented the feeling that he was being looked over as a possible future son-in-law. Then, too, he still felt it was ridiculous to even consider the possibility of marriage until he was out of school, and so there was no reason why he should try to impress them at all. Let them see just how poor he was.

"Yes," he said, "do you suppose I could get a little bag to put the extra food in. That is, unless you want it?"

Aware that he was probably losing points with Jenny's parents, but angry with their obvious wealth, Kevin dropped every spare morsel of food on the table into the bag the waitress had brought him. Once he looked up from his efforts to clear the table of food to see that Jenny was hurt by what he was doing—trying to discourage her parents from liking him.

A few minutes later, Jenny and her mother left the table to visit a store in the building.

Jenny's father ordered a second cup of coffee. "How do you think I got to be a banker?" he asked Kevin.

"I don't know."

"Hard work. I had to struggle through college the same as you. Don't ever be ashamed because things are tight."

Kevin found himself looking at Jenny's father with new admiration.

"It'll sharpen your goals and make you ten times more effective than if things had been easy."

"I appreciate you telling me that," Kevin said.

"Second, I don't think you're in any position to marry, do you?"

"No sir, I don't."

"Of course, Jenny hasn't mentioned it, but after spending all these years studying people who come in for a loan, one gets a little skill in observation, and I'd say you and she were in love."

"Yes."

"Marriage now isn't something I'd recommend. Maybe in a couple of years."

"I feel the same way," Kevin replied.

"Good. Don't make the same mistake we made. We were both headstrong and in love and got married when I was still in college. Can you picture me selling cookware on weekends and mopping floors in the morning? Or my wife working as a seamstress in a clothing store? She'd hate to admit it now, I think. Yes sir, don't make the same mistake."

"No, sir."

"Still," he said, his eyes wistful, "in some ways those were our happiest years."

A few days later, Kevin and Jenny went to have supper with Kevin's former missionary companion and his wife and baby. Harly and Janet Mitchell lived in the basement apartment of a home. The apartment had been hastily built a few years before, when the college appealed to local citizens to help meet the housing needs of a growing student enrollment. The furnace room was stuck in the middle of the apartment, and the ceiling was filled with air ducts carrying heat upstairs. A shower spout stood outside the bathroom in the kitchen, with only a plastic curtain and a drain. Harly explained that they also mopped the floor after every shower.

They had a casserole of macaroni and cream of mushroom soup, a plate of carrots, a bowl of peas, and a jello salad. But the hit of the evening was their six-month-old baby who stole the show.

"Oh, she's precious," Jenny said, holding the baby in her arms. "It's such a nice outfit for her too."

"Thanks to grandparents and friends," Janet said. "Because of them, she's taken care of for clothes."

A few minutes later, Harly asked the inevitable question. "What about you, Kevin? About time you got married, too."

"After I finish college," Kevin said firmly, his jaws set tightly.

Kevin and Jenny walked home afterwards at a quick pace.

"They have a beautiful baby, don't they?" she said.

"Every shred of clothes it has came from relatives," Kevin snapped.

"So?"

"So, I'm never going to be in a situation where my children have to depend on other people for clothes."

"Funny, the baby doesn't seem to mind," Jenny observed quietly.

"They are in no position financially to have a baby!" Kevin said, stopping to confront her.

"The General Authorities counsel that married couples shouldn't postpone having children, not even for schooling."

. "Then they shouldn't have married until he was through school."

"They love each other. Doesn't that count for anything? I'm sure they didn't want to wait for two years."

"What if the baby gets sick? What then?" Kevin asked harshly.

"Then Harly might have to quit school and get a job."

"And just throw away his schooling?"

"You're not really that concerned about the baby, are you?" she shot out.

"No, and this conversation's not really about them either, is it?"

She looked at him for a long time and then said, "No, I guess not."

"Jenny, I'm going to finish school in three years. Nothing's going to stand in my way."

"I see."

He didn't kiss her when he said good-bye at the dorm.

He didn't call her for three days after that.

Finally, unable to stand being apart, he phoned her and asked her to go with him to a Young Adult party that Friday night.

Everything went fine Friday until it came time for the entertainment. The girl in charge gathered everyone close to her in the cultural hall and announced a game. She asked the young people to take off their shoes and put them in a pile.

Kevin got up and quietly walked into the hall.

A minute later, Jenny joined him in the hall.

"Is anything wrong?" she asked.

"I have holes in my socks," he said quietly.

"Oh."

"I can't even afford a pair of socks."

Jenny touched his hand.

"All I've got for shirts are white shirts from my mission, but they're falling apart. This shirt has a big hole in the sleeve where my elbow has worn through, so with this shirt I always have to wear a sweater, and never take it off." He pulled the sleeve of the sweater to show her the ragged shape the shirt was in. "I've got slacks where the back is getting so thin that I have to wear a sport coat to hide the seat of the slacks."

"I love you, Kevin, not your socks."

"But don't you see, things aren't going to get any better for three more years."

"It'll be okay."

"Look, Jenny, I know I've avoided talking about us. I'd ask you to marry me, but how can I? I couldn't even afford the license."

She snuggled against him. "I'll chip in a couple of dollars," she whispered. "It's for a good cause."

"Your father doesn't want you marrying a guy who can't provide for you."

"It'd only be for a little while. I could quit school and work."

"You should finish your education."

Jenny stayed close to him, and he felt a tear fall from her cheek on his hand.

"There are too many *shoulds* in all this," she said.

"It's going to torment us all the time now," he said, stroking her hair. "I can't stand being away from you, and now I can't stand being with you. If we could just put things on hold for two years and then start it up again."

"How do we do that?" she asked.

As gently as he could, he said, "Maybe we shouldn't see each other for a while."

"Is that what you want?"

"No, but let's try it for a while."

He walked her to the dorm, said good-bye, and left.

The days that followed were terrible. He'd sit down to study and find himself looking at her picture 20 minutes later. Whenever he saw a phone, it haunted him, and he had to rush by so he wouldn't break down and phone her. He'd sit down to outline a chapter and find himself going over the figures estimating how much money he'd need to be able to marry her. The answer was always the same.

In church they could hardly stand to be in the same room. He offered his services to the bishop, hoping to be called to teach a Sunday School class so he wouldn't have to be in the Young Adult class with her.

Once he rounded a corner in church and found himself facing her.

"Hi, Jenny," he said brightly. "How are you?"

"Just fine," she countered quickly.

"Fine," he said breezily, but then his depression seeped out across his face. Instead of moving on, they stood there silently in the hall, staring at each other, both of them in agony.

"It's tough, isn't it?" he asked.

"Unbelievable," she replied.

Then he walked away.

He fasted and prayed. He called his father collect and asked for advice. Strangely enough, the answer came in a personal priesthood interview with his elders quorum president.

"Oh, Kevin before you go, would it be all right if we gave you another family to home teach? I just found out that Bill Morrill is graduating in May, so we need someone to pick up a couple of his families."

"Sure."

"Thanks. Boy, he's really had a good job while he's been in school. It's been perfect for him and his wife."

"What job is that?"

"Managing a motel."

Kevin pressed for more details, phoned up Bill Morill at the motel, visited with him the next day, and applied for the job. The owner hired him, starting in May.

Kevin phoned Jenny from a pay phone next to the motel, but her roommate said she'd gone away for the weekend and wouldn't be back until Sunday night.

He nearly went crazy waiting for Sunday to end. Between church meetings he spent his time writing a long list of ways to save money. Every possible idea was there. They'd drink straight powdered milk. They could get a free Christmas tree by asking some students in the dorm if they could have their tree when they went home for the holidays.

They'd save money for a room because a small apartment went with the job at the motel. At night all he had to do was man the desk and switchboard. He could get a lot of studying done at the same time. They'd never be able to afford a car, but they could get a small wagon to carry home the groceries from the store. They'd ask his aunt if they could help her with her garden during the summer in exchange for some vegetables.

Sunday evening after sacrament meeting he phoned her again.

"Hello," she said.

"We can get married!" he shouted.

There was a long pause, and then she said quietly, "I bet this is Kevin. Right?"

"How many other guys have you got about to propose?"

She laughed, and he said he'd be right over.

When she opened the door, he handed her his ten-page list.

"It's all there. We can do it."

She sat down and went over the list with him.

"It's very interesting," she said.

"That's all you can say?"

"What should I say?"

"Yes," he said.

"Yes to what?"

"Yes to my question."

"I didn't hear a question."

"WILL YOU MARRY ME?" he shouted, causing couples in the dorm to stop their conversation and stare at them.

"Yes," she laughed.

He kissed her.

A few minutes later they left the dorm to walk to their bishop's home.

"We'll be poor," he warned.

"No we won't," she said. "Not us. We won't be poor. We just won't have any money."

They walked quietly, holding hands, happy with the world.

"Wait a minute!" he said. "You haven't told me where you've been this weekend."

"I went home. My mother taught me how to mend socks."

Home Cooking

You're going to say I should have arranged housing in advance. But if I had, where would I be now?

After filling out a mountain of forms at registration, I drove around Provo looking for a place to stay. Finally I picked out one of the new apartment units near the campus. The office girl told me they had a vacancy in number 33.

The apartment complex is in the shape of a big C, with a swimming pool and frisby field in the middle. I walked across the lawn to number 33 and knocked on the screen door. Nobody came, although I could hear voices inside. I knocked again.

"Somebody get the door," a male voice yelled out.

I waited another minute and then knocked again. This time with my foot.

"Enrico, the door!"

A thin, antiseptic-looking guy shuffled to the door, holding a piece of chalk in his hand.

"Hi there," I said.

He gazed at me with a lost expression. "Hi," he mumbled, turning around and plodding back.

I opened the screen door and stepped in. The fellow with the chalk was writing on a chalkboard that someone had hung on the wall crooked. "The trouble was," he mumbled, "I'm not assuming a frictional air force. Let's try it again."

There was another student on the couch. He was reading a Russian newspaper out loud.

"Excuse me," I said. "Do you speak English?" He ignored me. Finally I turned to a fellow talking on the phone. "They said you had a vacancy. I need a room. Okay if I move in?"

He waved me away with one arm. "I know the concert was arranged, but the drummer got sick. So no concert. Do you follow that much?"

A girl walked in carrying a sack of groceries and three shirts rolled up in a plastic bag. She set the groceries on the kitchen counter, got an ironing board and iron from a closet. Pulling out one of the damp shirts from the bag, she started to press it.

"Look," the guy on the phone continued, "if there's no concert, then we don't need the popcorn we ordered from you for refreshments. It's that simple." He paused, listening to the man at the other end. "I know I ordered 200 pounds of popcorn. But that was when I thought the band would be here." He started walking around the room, gesturing to add emphasis. "No, I don't know how much space 200 pounds of popcorn takes up." Pause. "That much?" "No, I don't know what you're going to do with it."

That's the way it was. The fellow at the chalkboard, who I later learned is named Harold Roberts, is a physics major and nicknamed Enrico, after Enrico Fermi the famous World War II scientist. He was writing down line after line of equations, talking excitedly as he went. The second fellow is Roger Thornton, who we call Boris because he's a Russian language major. He was reading *Pravda*. The third guy, Brad Jones, called B.J., is a studentbody officer majoring in pre-law. The girl, Cher Weiss, had a classic Greek face with high cheek bones and a dominant nose. She was wearing a pair of wire frame glasses. Her dark, shoulder-length hair fell in front of her face as she worked and was periodically being brushed aside.

I walked over to the girl. "Excuse me, do you speak English?"

"What's that supposed to mean?"

"Talk to me, please. Nobody else will."

"Aren't you working with Enrico?"

"No. I just want to talk about the vacancy."

"All right, have it your way," B.J. said. "We'll pay for the popcorn at half price. Goodbye." He slammed down the phone, immediately picked it up again, and dialed.   He walked over to the girl and touched the finished shirt hanging on the doorknob. "Not so much starch next time, Cher."

"This guy wants to talk to you," she said to B.J., who finally hung up because the line was busy.

"If it's about the concert, we'll refund the money at the Wilkinson Center desk starting Monday."

"It's about the vacancy. I want to move in."

"I'm in a hurry now," B.J. said as he picked up the shirt hanging on the doorknob and started for a bedroom. "It's okay by me if you move in. Did they tell you how much the rent is?"

"Right."

"Okay. We've got a phone. That's extra. Cher comes in each day and cooks our supper for us. We each pay $10 a week, and she buys all our groceries and takes a little something for herself. That's it. Take it or leave it."

"I'll take it," I said.

"Okay. Sure great to meet you," he said as he disappeared into his room.

I shook hands with Boris and Enrico, although they didn't realize why for a couple of days.

B.J. came out of his room, wearing the neatly pressed shirt, a tie, and a blazer. "Well, see you later," he said to nobody in particular on his way out.

Boris put on a pair of large, wraparound, stereo headphones and sat down on the couch, listening to Russian tapes. Enrico got his equations about two-thirds of the way down the chalkboard and then ran out of steam. He stood there, examining the first equation and its logical, muddy conclusion.

I brought in my luggage and deposited it in the room with the empty bed. After unpacking and washing up, I went back out into the living room-kitchen combination.

"I've got a few shirts that need ironing too," I said to Cher. "There's no hurry though."

"Take them to the cleaners. I'm not in the business."

"Sorry, I thought it was part of the service," I explained.

"It isn't. I just iron B.J.'s shirts."

Oh. Why does he get special treatment?"

"I don't know," she said, hanging up the second shirt. "Sometimes I wonder."

"Are you going together?"

"We used to. We still go out sometimes, but not much anymore. He's so busy with student politics and all."

"What year in school are you?" I asked.

"Senior."

"Me too. Feels great to be almost out, right?"

"Negative," she replied.

"How come?"

"I'm not engaged or married. If you're a fellow and that happens, you're just choosy. But if you're a girl, they say, 'Four years in a school with 8,000 boys and she couldn't find one?' "

"Who's they?" I asked.

I don't know." she looked up and smiled. "Sorry. Forget what I said."

"Sure. Are your folks members?"

"There's just my dad now. Mom died two years ago. I joined the Church when I was 14. But Daddy is still about as far away as you can get from joining the Church. How about you?"

"I joined the Church just last year," I explained. "My parents still think we're the group with the nice neat farms in Pennsylvania."

"What will you do when you graduate?" I asked.

"Go back home. That's Patchogue, New York. Or else get a job in an office building in Salt Lake and set traps in the hall."

"Patchogue. That's on the island, isn't it?" I asked.

"Yes, have you been there?"

Sure, it's on the way to Riverhead, Right? I was raised in Queens until I was 16, and then we moved to Trucksville, Pennsylvania."

"No kidding," Cher said, putting away the ironing board and iron. "I thought you spoke nice. Out west they have a dialect all their own." She went into the kitchen area and took some cans out of the bag. "I'm waiting for the day Daddy comes out for graduation. He has a New York accent you can cut with a knife. I can just hear him, 'Tirty tousand people, and an old man can't get a cup of coffee?' "

We talked about how we came to be taught the gospel, and the changes it had made in our lives.

"What are we having for supper?"

"Steak, tossed salad, and strawberry shortcake."

"How do you cook like that on what we're giving you and still make a profit?"

"I shop bargains," she said, her face clouding over.

I stood in the kitchen and watched her work. I added up in my head the cost of the food for that meal alone. It was expensive.

"Cher, how much are you kicking in to the food bill?"

She turned around. "Not much. Really."

"Is it to impress B.J.?"

"Don't tell him. Okay?"

She explained that she had met B.J. her first semester. They were in the same branch. She helped him run for freshman class president. They went steady until he went on his mission.

"Once he asked me to marry him before he left. I said I would. I waited for two years until he got back. I even changed my major twice so I would not be ahead of him in school when he returned. We dated some after he got back, and then he got interested in campus politics again. He's forgotten I'm around now. It's like I'm not really here."

She seemed to get so depressed talking about B.J. that I changed the subject. "Tell me something. After you're here for a while, don't you miss the New York taxi drivers, delicatessens, and Jones Beach?"

"When I joined the Church all of a sudden I wanted to be Mormon in everything. I learned to make quilts, can pickles, and make plastic grapes at Relief Society. I want the whole package— a father-in-law who's on the high council, a mother-in-law who makes bread, and a crowd of relatives who get together every year in Emigration Canyon for a reunion."

The steak was ready at six. B.J. came in 45 minutes late.

"Why are you late?" I asked.

"I had a meeting. Why, did I miss something?"

"No. Cher has gone to all this trouble to prepare a nice supper, and you come back with the steak all dried out and cold."

"It tastes okay," he said, washing down the steak with a glass of milk.

"Okay? Is that all you can say? This is not a hamburger and fries at some roadside diner. Tell Cher you like it."

"I like it Cher. Well, I've got to run."

"Have some dessert," I demanded.

"I don't have time."

"What? The school is suddenly going to fall apart if you don't leave now. Have some dessert."

"I'll have it when I get back," B.J. said.

"The whipped cream will be turned back into a puddle at the bottom of the bowl by then."

"What are you, the Galloping Gourmet?"

"It just seems that you could show a little appreciation around here. That's all."

"We're paying her to cook for us whether I eat it or not."

"It's okay, Tony," Cher said. "Get off B.J.'s back. It's no big deal."

B.J. went into his room. Boris went out. Enrico erased the chalkboard and began the ritual of filling it with funny symbols. I helped Cher clean up.

In a few minutes B. J. came out wearing another neatly pressed shirt. His face was shaved and covered with after shave lotion. "See you around."

"Where are you going?" I asked.

"I've got a date to study political science."

I dried while Cher washed the dishes. We didn't speak for awhile.

"It doesn't hurt you that he's wearing one of the shirts you washed, starched, and ironed on his date? You know, he's making the big impression with your creases."

"I know. Let's not talk about it."

"And that doesn't bother you?"

"Only when there's lipstick on the collar." She looked like she was going to cry.

"I'm not going to let it go on this way. Either give him up or do something different. May I suggest giving him up?"

She concentrated on scrubbing the broiler pan. Finally she said quietly, "Let's talk about doing something different."

We finished the dishes and sat down around the kitchen table. I took out a sheet of notebook paper and wrote at the top "Operation Engagement."

"We'll make a list of the things a fellow looks for in an LDS girl. First: testimony. Second: a nice face, a good figure. Third: common interests. Fourth: sense of humor. Fifth: a supporting attitude."

"Let's go down the list," Cher said. "Testimony. I've got one, Tony. I really do."

"Okay," I said, putting down a check on the paper.

"Face." She held out her hand rotating it to the right and then to the left in a gesture familiar to Easterners. "I don't know. What do you think?"

"It's very good. Like a Greek goddess. Do you have many cavities?"

"Our water had fluoride—53% fewer cavities."

I put a check beside "Face."

"Wait," she said, "except for the glasses."

"You have to see."

"I'll get contact lens."

"I like you the way you are."

"It's not you we're trying to impress," she said cooly. Then, quickly, "I'm sorry, that wasn't kind."

"No problem."

"Figure?"

I cleared my throat. "Fine."

"You don't think I'm too skinny?"

"No, ma'am."

"Aren't you going to say anything more about the figure?"

"No, ma'am."

"Do I dress modestly enough?"

"You dress like a lady."

"Maybe I should dress less modestly to get B.J.'s attention."

"If he noticed you that way, I'd punch him out."

"Okay. Common interests," she said.

"I think B.J.'s biggest interest is himself. So you have a common interest."

"You don't know him very well. Be constructive."

"Okay," I replied. "Boys from the West are crazy about deer hunting. Do you know anything about deer hunting?"

"What's there to know?" she asked.

"Do you know how to clean a deer?"

"Do they get dirty?"

"I will ignore that. Probably your biggest common interest is the Church. Maybe that's enough. Let's see, sense of humor."

"I don't think B. J. has a sense of humor."

"If you marry him, you're going to need one. A supporting attitude. That means you help him on his campaigns. Or you try to do nice things for him, like cooking his favorite food to show him that he's special to you. You're doing fine, Cher."

"Tony, there's one other thing. I have some of that Eastern cynicism. I'm not like your average coed. Maybe I seem too cynical. I need to be more sincere." She wrote down another word at the bottom of the list, sincerity.

The next afternoon when I came in after my lab, she was already working on supper.

"Tony, look what I picked up in the bookstore today. You're not going to believe this. It's perfume in a time-release capsule. You just open this little pill and scatter the tiny beads on your hair with this little can. The beads are programmed. The aroma starts out kind of mild, but in about three hours it's something. I'm going to put some on."

She applied the contents of one of the small capsules.

"Do you want to smell?"

"In the interests of science," I said.

"Let's see. It's 4:30 now. We'll eat at 6:00. So if I can get around B. J. by 7:00, I'll give him the full dose."

She started peeling potatoes. I sat at the table and thumbed through a book I was supposed to be reading. The perfume did change aroma as time went on.

"I pick up my contact lenses on Monday, Tony. And I've really worked at being sincere. Look at me."

She was standing with her head up, looking at the ceiling.

"What are you looking at the ceiling for?

"I'm looking at the clouds as the sun breaks through."

"We're in a room. There are no clouds," I said.

"I know. But you've seen those movies where they close with someone looking at the clouds. Now that's a sincere look, right? Well, I've got it, right?"

I stood up, grabbed a dish towel, and draped it over her sincere face.

Later, after we had cleaned up the water she had thrown on me, we got back to work.

"Tony, what if this doesn't work out? I think if I hear one more talk about the importance of marriage and the family, I will cry. I'm doing the best I can."

B.J. was on time. He complimented Cher on the meal too.

"How's our campus leader?" I asked him.

"Busy. Next week we go to the Church Office Building with the Belle of the Y. We'll see some of the General Authorities and then have our picture taken."

"That's really great, B.J.," Cher said as she leaned down by him, ostensibly to look at his appointment book but really to allow him a whiff of "T + Three Hours and Counting" perfume.

It was at that moment I realized I loved Cher and didn't want her to be around B.J.

Monday when I came in, Cher had her contact lenses.

"So how do you like me now?"

"You can really see me?"

"Sure."

"But why are you crying?" I asked.

"My eyes are just watering a little. It'll clear up once I get used to the lenses."

"I can't even see them on you. Let me get a little closer." I moved very close to her and looked into her eyes.

"How's that?" she asked.

"Fine."

"I mean, can you see them now?"

"I'll have to get closer."

"That's close enough," she said, moving away.

"Are they hard to take out?"

"Not at all. You just put your finger here on the corner of your eye and blink." She put her other hand below her eye, but the lens missed her hand and fell to the floor.

"Just stay there, Cher. I'll look for it." I got down on my hands and knees and started looking for it. I soon found the small, green, plastic lens. "Cher, can you see anything?"

"No. Why?"

"Nothing." I put the lens in my shirt pocket.

"Cher, maybe if you get down and help look for it."

She got down on her hands and knees also. "I think we should both concentrate our efforts over here where you were when you dropped it." I moved over by her.

We looked and looked. Finally we decided to take it one tile at a time.

"Tony? You have your hand on top of my hand," she said, looking down at our hands.

"Oh, I do. Do you want me to move it, Cher?"

"I don't know. I can't decide."

"Cher, you are really good looking."

"With contacts, I'll look better. Maybe that's been my trouble all along."

"No, I mean with glasses, and without the time-release perfume, and without the forced sincere look. You are beautiful. You don't need any improvement."

"No, I'm not beautiful."

"Yes, you are."

"No, I'm not," she insisted.

"Yes, you are."

"No, I'm not."

"Well, maybe not beautiful. But definitely pretty."

"So you don't think I'm beautiful!"

"Yes, I do. But you wouldn't accept it, so I figured I'd compromise. And Cher, you are sincere. In fact, you are just about the most sincere person I've ever met. Truly."

"Thank you. I try to be sincere. And Tony, you're the only person I've ever been able to talk to without wondering what I'm supposed to say. With you I'm just myself."

"Cher, you have a nice hand."

"We shouldn't be here alone like this."

"We're not alone, Cher. Boris is on the couch, and Enrico is looking at the chalkboard.

"I know," she whispered, "but it's like being along."

"Cher, you are very special to me."

"I don't want to hurt you, Tony."

"Who's hurting? My knees are a little sore, that's all."

"That's not what I meant. I don't want you to fall in love with me."

"It's too late. I already have. I want to marry you, and I'm asking you."

She started crying.

"If you want to wait before you give me an answer, that's okay."

I got up to get her a box of tissues. When I returned, she was sitting on the chair in the kitchen. She wiped her eyes, blew her nose, and sat there.

"Tony, I really like you, but I've been thinking about B.J. for so long there's no more room for anyone else in my heart. Can we be good friends?"

The next day I paid a visit to B.J.'s office in the Wilkinson Center. "B.J., I want to talk to you."

I told him about Cher and the way she felt about him. "The poor girl," he said. "I had no idea she felt so strongly about me."

"What are you going to do about it?" I asked him.

"I guess I'll have to take my shirts to the cleaners and tell her to buzz off."

I slammed my hand down on his desk, breaking his plastic, desk name plate. "No, B.J., that's not what you're going to do. You're going to take that girl out and try to fall in love with her. You are going to treat her like a queen, or some morning you're going to wake up with your head shaved."

"Perhaps I should go out with her," he said quietly.

For the next several weeks, I stayed clear of Cher. I spent my late afternoons watching the Foucault pendulum swing, or listening to music, or taking long walks. Then I would go home around 8:00 and eat whatever was left. Cher was cooking for B.J. now. She made homemade wheat bread, beef stew, meatloaf—the things that B.J. liked.

It was especially bad when I knew they were going out, and I stayed away from campus for fear I'd see them together. Every couple seen from a distance looked like them. Every time I saw a girl with her head on some boy's shoulder, I got cold chills. I wished I had never met her.

One weekend B.J. took Cher home with him to meet the family. That was the Saturday I ran. I got up early and put on sweat pants and sweat shirt and drove out to a country road. After parking the car I started running. Soon there was just the road, the pain in my side, and the crunch of my feet against the gravel. But the pain in my side increased. So I kept on. Finally I collapsed on the side of the road. It was a long time before I could make myself get up and walk back to the car.

A couple of weeks later B.J. had to go to a conference of student leaders in New Mexico. That Tuesday night I entered the apartment at 8:00 expecting to see the usual empty kitchen with a plate of food in the refrigerator.

Cher was in the kitchen cooking. "I thought you were never coming," she said. "Sit down and get started."

She sat down across from me, and we said the blessing.

We got through the salad in silence. Removing the salad plate, she replaced it with a plate of lasagna and garlic bread.

"Why are you cooking with B.J. gone?"

"I get paid to cook here, remember?"

"But why did you wait for me? I'm two hours late."

"Your name Tony Versalino? Of Italian ancestry? You like Italian food?"

"Yes."

"That's what it means."

"Cher?"

"Item five, a supporting attitude. 'Like cooking his favorite food.' "

I put down my fork and held her hand. "What about B.J.?"

"He was a dream in my mind for all those years, but a dream with no reality. Besides, it finally occurred to me that it wasn't necessary for all members of the Church to walk and talk and live like they came from Panguitch, Provo, or Parowan. I can't fit the Utah-Mormon mold. I like the East, and I want to go back and help the Church grow there."

"You mean, the West is a nice place to visit, but you wouldn't want to live there?" I caught the aroma of her perfume in the last stages of its time-release cycle. "Lady, what you need is a nice Mormon boy from Pennsylvania."

"I don't want to push you, Tony."

"I'm your man."

"You know what Daddy is going to say?" Cher said. " 'Queens? He's from Queens? I send you by plane across the country, you live in a desert for years, and you find a husband from Queens? For Queens, I could pay subway fare. Now you tell me you want to get married in a temple in Utah? We got plenty of temples in New York, and I know a rabbi . . .' "

For dessert we had a dish of Italian ice.

The Least of These, My Brother

The class bell rang, and a few stragglers darted quickly into their classrooms, leaving Jed Fischer stranded in a new school with a locker that wouldn't open. For the fifth time he slowly turned through the numbers written on a slip of paper, but it wouldn't open.

"What are you doing in the hall during class time?" a voice sternly barked behind him.

He turned, expecting to face an angry teacher, but instead found a girl his age sporting an impish grin.

"Scared you, didn't I?" Her face was freckled and she had short, tossled, reddish-brown hair. Plopping her books in his arms, she took the paper giving his combination. After dialing the three numbers, she slammed the locker with her foot. The locker flew open.

"It sticks. You have to hit it." She opened her own locker, next to his, and took her books from him.

"Thanks," he said. "I just transferred here from Idaho."

"Welcome to New York. I'm Pam Burgess."

"My name is Jed Fischer."

"I know. I work in the office in the afternoon. My family is very big for volunteer work," she said, with a touch of sarcasm in her voice. "I looked at your records when you came here. I found out that you're a junior, that your dad is a nuclear engineer transferred from Idaho to Brookhaven Lab, and that you're a football player. Are you a Mormon?"

"Yes."

"Then you're the only one in this school."

"My sister goes here too. She's a sophomore. So there're two Mormons."

"What's her name?"

"Brenda."

"Does she have curly hair like her brother?" Pam asked.

"No. That's the curse of our family. The girls have straight hair."

"Do you want to walk around, and I'll give you the tour?" Pam asked, closing her locker.

"What about you?" he asked as they leisurely strolled the halls.

"My mom and dad both work in the city. Mom is in advertising. Dad's a stockbroker. I see him about twice a month."

They passed the cafeteria. The smell of tuna fish casserole invaded the hall.

"Nobody eats there," she said.

"Somebody must."

"Oh, sure, the losers."

"Who are the losers?" he asked.

"There are just two kinds of people in the world, the winners and the losers. Didn't you know that? You look to me like a winner."

"Where do the winners eat?" he asked.

"We go to a little pizza place a couple of blocks from here. I'll meet you at noon and show you."

He met Pam at noon. They were joined by one other boy, Doug Cabot, who spent his time complaining about how rotten everything was.

The pizza shop was old. Two large fans resembling airplane propellers stuck from the ceiling. At noon the place was crowded with kids from school. All the booths were being used, and several people were jammed around the stand-up counter. After they had ordered, they stood and waited.

"I think we can sit down over there," Doug said, looking at a small booth near the corner.

They walked over to the booth. There was just one boy in the booth. He was overweight and wore a pair of thick glasses that seemed to magnify his eyes to an observer. He ate his pizza without looking up, avoiding eye contact with any person in the room.

"Ernie, how's it going?" Doug asked, his voice conveying a mood of cruelty.

The boy looked up with a weak smile.

"We saw you sitting all alone in this big booth, and we thought you might be nearly through."

Ernie understood the threat. "You can sit here. I'm almost finished."

Ernie stood up, grabbing his cardboard platter with pizza still on it, and started to leave the booth. Doug stood in his way.

"You sure gorge yourself, Ernie," Doug said. "What's it like to be fat? Since you have such a weight problem, would you mind if we borrowed a couple of slices to nibble on until our order is done?" Doug reached out and took a slice.

"Give him back his pizza, Doug," Jed said firmly.

"Why? He's letting me have it."

"Leave him alone."

"Are you a friend of his?" Doug asked. "Because if you are, you're the only one he's got."

Pam broke the mounting tension. "Lay off, Doug. Our pizza is done."

Doug stepped aside for Ernie to pass. About halfway to the door, somebody deliberately bumped Ernie's arm and his pizza fell on the floor. Ernie knelt down, scraped up the mess, and threw it in the garbage can on his way out.

During lunch, Doug talked about the injustices committed against a group of people in South America.

Jed found out when he went to class that Pam was in his chemistry class. On that day they were having a lab. Each group was given a test tube with an unknown solution in it. The purpose of the lab was to determine what the unknown was by performing a series of chemical tests.

Pam invited Jed to work with her. "Nothing to it," she smiled. She walked to the checkout counter in the back of the room and started talking to the lab assistant. The others in the class were testing for the unknown.

In a few minutes Pam came back with a slip of paper. "I found out what our unknown is. Just copy this down on your lab notebook."

"What about the tests we're supposed to perform?" Jed asked.

"All the reactions are negative except numbers 3 and 11."

"Aren't we going to do it?"

"What for? This is how I do all the experiments. If you want to be a hero and smell like hydrochloric acid, be my guest."

Jed sheepishly signed his name to the report and turned it in.

As they walked downstairs to their lockers, she suggested driving to Montauk Point on the tip of Long Island.

She let him drive her car, a late model sports car. When they arrived, the wind was whipping up white caps on the incoming waves. The turbulent waves smashed against huge boulders, sending up geysers of spray.

They walked along a path that climbed up to a rocky precipice. Near the top they found a place where they could sit and watch the endless water.

"Most people come here in the summer," she said, her arms wrapped around her legs. "Sometimes it seems like there are a million, and every one of them has a bag of potato chips and a bottle of suntan lotion. They gobble the chips, throw the bag on the beach, douse themselves with oil, and fry."

They watched the clouds changing shapes as they swept across the sky.

"I like to come in the winter," she continued, "after the wind and the breakers have ripped away all the debris, leaving it clean."

She pointed out to him the silhouette of a freighter on the horizon.

"Hard to believe all this is an accident," she said, observing the harsh beauty of the ocean.

"It didn't just happen."

"You seem sure of yourself."

"I am," he replied.

"Back in school or at home, I really get so I don't care about God. But sometimes, when I walk here, there's a feeling I get. It's hard to explain, but a feeling that He's there somewhere. But by the time I'm back in my car and stuck in the traffic on the freeway, the feeling is gone."

He studied her face as she talked. She was beautiful even with the wind scattering her hair. He felt as if he cared for her, not really like being her boyfriend, but more like a brother. It was a good, clean feeling, and he thought that she felt it too.

"Pam, I want to tell you about my church."

They made a date for her to attend his ward on Sunday. When they returned to the car, the feeling was gone.

"Well, that turned into a real prayer group, didn't it?" she said, embarrassed.

They made it back to his home at 7:30. Luckily his parents had gone out that night to have dinner with his father's new boss. While Jed got out of the car, Pam slid over to the driver's side, smiled, and drove away. When he walked in the house, his sister Brenda was standing at the window.

"Well, I don't have to ask you how your first day of school went," she teased. She was tall and graceful, looking like she could be a ballet dancer. Yet at home she preferred levis and an old long-sleeved shirt of Jed's. The hardest thing about the move for her had been the sale of her quarter horse.

"Her name is Pam, and I think she's interested in the Church."

"Where have you been?"

"We went to Montauk Point. How was your day?"

"Not too bad, considering I don't know anybody in the school."

The next day after English class, Ernie walked over to Jed and said, "Thanks for trying to help me yesterday." His eyes darted up to Jed's face and then down again, uncertain of his standing.

"Sure."

"They say you're a Mormon. I've got an uncle who's a Mormon. He joined a year ago. Is there a Mormon church on the island?"

"Several."

"Can people who aren't members go to it?"

"Yes." Jed inwardly cringed at the thought of Pam seeing Ernie at church.

"I'd like to go this Sunday. My uncle keeps telling me how friendly the people are."

"You can't smoke on church property," Jed said coolly.

"I know. I have a jacket with these pants. Is that okay to wear?"

Jed looked at the wrinkled, gray dress slacks with tiny cuffs. They must be ten years old, he thought to himself. "I guess so," he said dryly.

It was only the second time that Jed had been to church in New York. After priesthood meeting he was in the hall putting on his jacket so that he could drive out to pick up Pam. Ernie walked in. His forehead was sweating, and he was puffing.

Elder Baker, one of the missionaries assigned to the ward, rushed Ernie shortly after he walked in, shaking his hand and welcoming him to church.

Jed reluctantly came out from the coat rack area and said hello to Ernie. "I see you made it," he said. Ernie rambled on about missing an exit and going three miles out of his way. Jed looked nervously at his watch and excused himself.

Pam's home was a three-story brick house set on a hill overlooking Long Island Sound. A maid answered Jed's ring and showed him to the den. He sat and studied the wall of bookshelves; in the middle of the room was a large, natural-stone fireplace.

In a few minutes Pam appeared. It was the first time he had seen her dressed up. She looked beautiful and rich.

"What's it going to be like?" she asked on the way. "Will you help me so I'll know when to kneel or what to say?"

"It's not like that. It's very simple. More like a big family than anything. In fact, we teach that we're all brothers and sisters. So if anyone calls you Sister Burgess, don't faint."

He took the exit from the freeway. "Oh, Pam, there's one other thing. That fat kid, Ernie, cornered me in class, and well, he's going to be in church too."

She looked at him with raised eyebrows. "Ernie?"

They got there late. Jed saw the elders taking Ernie to the investigator's class, and so he decided to take Pam to the class for high school students.

Sacrament meeting was held immediately after Sunday School. It seemed extra long to Jed. The high council visitor was there. He talked about welfare and explained how he used to hoe sugar beets on a welfare farm in Utah as a boy. Jed counted him using poor grammar ten times during the talk. A young mother in front of them struggled with her two-year-old boy, feeding him soda crackers one at a time. Jed felt embarrassed about church for the first time in his life.

On the way home Pam talked enthusiastically about their summer home in Maine and how she'd like him to see it sometime when her folks took her there.

"Thanks," she said as they pulled up in her driveway.

"I guess it seemed a little different from the church you usually go to," he said.

"Yes, it did."

"I'm sorry about the noise."

"That's okay. I guess it's what you get used to."

"Will you let the missionaries explain about our beliefs?"

She grinned. "I'm more interested in you than I am in your church."

"It means a lot to me."

"I'll see," she answered.

When Jed got home, Elder Baker and his companion were there.

"Ernie's really ready for the gospel!" Elder Baker announced. "He wants to have the discussions. It'd be great if we could have them here so he could be fellowshipped."

Jed's mother agreed, and they arranged the first discussion for Tuesday evening.

"How about inviting the girl you brought to church to hear the lessons at the same time?"

"No, not with Ernie."

The discussion on Tuesday was a success as far as the missionaries were concerned. After Ernie had left, Elder Baker said, "He'll be baptized. Jed, you can really help him by fellowshipping. Eat lunch with him, take him to activity night, get to be friends with him."

"A guy like that will never join the Church," Jed said grimly.

"What do you mean by that?" his father challenged.

"Nothing," Jed said, unwilling to get into an argument.

The next week Jed started on the next chemistry lab experiment, determined to quit his reliance on Pam's friendship with the student lab assistant. He was still reading the complicated directions when Pam came back to where he was working.

"Sodium hydroxide," she whispered in his ear.

"Go away. I'm busy."

"The unknown is sodium hydroxide. But now that I've told you, it's not unknown, is it? I've saved you two hours of work. Will you come home with me and help me fix my ten-speed?"

After they'd looked at the bike, she gave him a piece of cake. They sat and ate in the kitchen. The kitchen floor looked like it could have been used for a commercial about floor wax.

"My dad says he knew a Mormon in the service; he respects them."

"Did you ask him about taking the missionary lessons?"

"I never ask him anything unless it costs money," she answered.

"Well, are you going to take them?"

"I don't know. Is it all that important?"

"Yes, it is."

"Is good old Ernie going to be a Mormon?" she teased.

"No."

"If he did, you'd have to call him Brother Ernie, wouldn't you? And if I joined too, he'd call me Sister Pam. That'd be great," she said cynically. "He's a loser, Jed. Face it."

That Friday night Pam's parents took Jed and Pam to dinner with them in Manhattan. They ate at a Japanese restaurant where they removed their shoes and ate on bamboo mats in a small enclosed room. Afterwards they went to a Broadway play. They talked during intermission about inviting him to see their summer cabin in Maine.

The next week the elders persuaded Jed to pick up Ernie for activity night. He and his mother lived in a housing development built for low-income people. Ernie's mother was a tired-looking woman with a deep, hacking smoker's cough.

They played volleyball that night. At first Ernie was just going to watch, but Brenda talked him into playing on her side. She stood next to him and instructed him about how to set up the ball for players in the front row to spike. When he missed, which he did frequently, she'd say, "That's okay, Ernie," or, "Nice try." By the end of the first game, he was returning most of the serves hit to him. By the end of the second game, he was excited about the game, encouraging other players, and shouting when they gained a point.

Jed and Brenda drove him home after it was over. He joked with Brenda about his poor eyesight, telling how he stepped on his glasses once while he was looking for them. Jed was silent.

After they had let Ernie out at his home, Brenda started in with Jed. "The only time you paid any attention to Ernie was when you spiked the ball toward him."

"He was the weakest member of your team. It was just good strategy."

"You aren't helping him any."

"You're wasting your time, Brenda. He'll never join the Church."

"But your precious Pam will?"

"Yes, in time she will."

"My big brother is a dummy."

"My little sister can't face reality."

"Jed, why do you ignore him?"

"How can anybody ignore him? He's got bad breath."

"Do you think you're better than he is?" she asked.

"That's not the point. If I can get Pam interested in the Church, the Church will be made stronger. She knows a lot of people. But she'll never even look at the Church if Ernie is baptized."

"So you're just going to let Ernie go. His only chance, maybe, to hear the truth."

"I picked him up tonight. Isn't that enough?"

She was quiet for several minutes, and then, quietly, she asked, "What would the Savior do?"

"You're not going to trap me," Jed answered brusquely.

"Just tell me what He would do."

"It's more complicated than that. You don't understand. If I get tied up with Ernie, I won't have a friend in that whole school."

"Because he's fat."

"Yes, and sloppy and clumsy."

"Jed, you're my big brother. I used to be proud of you, but I'm not sure that I like you very much anymore. You've changed. Pam's changing you. Did you know that?"

"Tough," Jed said angrily.

The next Monday when Pam and Jed met at their lockers, she invited him to come with her and her family for the weekend while they did some work on the cabin in Maine. The plans called for them to fly up Friday and return on Monday afternoon.

His parents were not happy about the plan. "You're going to be missing two days of school. You're already behind," his mother said.

"What will you do about church on Sunday?" his dad asked.

"I don't know. Maybe I'll have to miss one time. It won't kill me."

"That's not the point. Where are your priorities?" his dad asked.

After an hour's discussion his dad finally said that Jed was getting old enough to make his own decisions, that he'd been taught what was right, and that he would be allowed to make his own decision.

Jed went to his room, knowing what he should decide, knowing what he was going to decide. After an hour of listening to his tapes, he walked downstairs and announced simply, "I'm going this weekend."

The next night Elder Baker and his companion came over and announced that Ernie was to be baptized Saturday. "And he wants you to baptize him, Jed."

There was an uneasy silence in the room. "I can't," Jed said. "I'm going with Pam and her parents to Maine for the weekend."

"Oh," Elder Baker said, looking at Jed's parents.

The next day at school Jed decided the least he could do was to explain to Ernie why he wouldn't be able to baptize him on Saturday.

"I'm sorry I can't go to your baptism. Pam's parents asked me up to their summer home in Maine."

"Do you think you might be falling in love with her?" Ernie asked.

"What's that to you?" Jed shot back.

"Nothing, I guess. Are you falling in love with her way of life?"

"Why?"

"I've got a friend in chemistry who says you and Pam are cheating."

"Just on the labs," Jed defended.

"Oh, just on the labs. I'll be sure to tell him. I'm sure he'll be much more interested in learning about the Church when I tell him you're only cheating on the labs."

"I'm going to make it up."

"I don't know if he'll believe that, but I'll tell him."

Jed felt his face flush with embarrassment. "Anything else? I'm in a hurry."

"Yes, one other thing," Ernie replied, looking straight at Jed. "I guess you're upset about my joining the Church, aren't you?"

"No," Jed said. "The Church is for everyone."

"But you'd like to choose which of those everyones joins, wouldn't you? A rich man, or a beautiful girl, and athlete, a talented artist, an influential politician. I'm not any of those things, am I? Do you think there's room in your church for me?"

Jed felt stunned as if he'd been hit.

"For the first time in my life, I now have a reason to live. But you've always had that, haven't you? It was very comfortable, wasn't it? Having the truth while the rest of us stumbled in the dark. I'd like to know how you feel, Jed. Not that it matters, I guess, because I'm going to be baptized. Not because of your example, but in spite of it."

Jed walked away. His face felt as if it were on fire.

He walked to a park, sat on a deserted park swing, and thought.

He went back at noon, ate in the cafeteria with Brenda, and for the first time they were able to talk again. After his last class, he met Pam at her locker.

"Pam, something has come up. I won't be able to go with your family this weekend."

"What's wrong?" she asked.

"I'm going to baptize Ernie Saturday."

"That's more important than being with us in Maine?"

"Tell your parents I'm sorry."

"I can't believe you'd back out of this trip just so you can baptize that clown Ernie."

"He's my brother."

"Then you're a loser too," she snapped, slamming her locker and walking away.

"Pam?" he called, when she was no more than 20 feet away.

She turned around, tearful yet defiant.

"Nobody's born a loser. We make the losers, you and me, by the way we treat them. We carefully mold them each day of their lives. But to the Savior, nobody's a loser."

She shook her head, turned away, and walked quickly down the long hall.

Jed watched her go and then slowly walked up the stairs for what became a long conversation with his chemistry teacher.

Sometimes a Phone Call

On Scott's 16th birthday, his father entered Scott's room and, clearing off a stack of oboe music from a chair so he could sit down, said, "Okay, you've been asking us to let you date Pam. You're 16 now. So go ahead and ask her out."

"I'm not ready to date yet," Scott said.

"But that's all you've talked about for a solid year," his father replied.

"I'm sorry, but a guy just can't rush into something like that. I'll date Pam when I'm ready."

His father left, shaking his head, wishing he understood his son. Scott tried to get ready to date Pam, but he had known her for four years and couldn't remember when she hadn't made him nervous. Even when he was 12 at a Scout-Beehive class breakfast, he'd dropped his pancakes when she asked him if he'd show her how to tie a square knot.

He spent hours thinking about how he'd ask her out. Every morning when he delivered a newspaper to her family's porch, he looked to see if he might discover a fire in the house from which he could rescue her and the whole family. He imagined her saying, "Oh, how can I ever repay you?" and he would say, "Ma'am, if you'd go with me to the stake youth dance, that'd be repayment enough."

Every night he'd take the hall phone with the long cord into his room and close the door. With great care he'd position the phone exactly in the center of the desk. Then he would stare at it. As a warm-up to phoning Pam, he'd dial the time-of-day number and talk to the recorded voice, concentrating on lowering his voice.

He'd become sensitive about his voice when he realized that most of the other guys in the priests group were singing bass and he was still singing the melody. In the morning when he delivered papers, he sometimes put pebbles in his mouth and yelled to the dogs who chased him along the route. He tried to imitate as much as possible what John Wayne, with pebbles in his mouth, would say to dogs chasing him if he delivered papers on a secondhand, one-speed bike.

Once he dialed Pam's number completely. When Pam answered, he cleared his throat and hung up, his face covered with perspiration.

In order to earn money for a karate course, complete with illustrated instruction manual and phonograph records (the course was guaranteed to build confidence), he found a summer job at the Dairy Dip Drive-in. He worked from 10:00 in the morning to 5:00 in the afternoon.

He worked with Becky Williams. It was apparent from the first that they would be "just friends" because she was taller than Scott—his eyes came level with her chin—she was older than he—17 compared with 16—she had little interest in the oboe, and she had a hot-tempered steady named Joe Kruglak who had gained local fame as a fighter. Joe worked as a mechanic in a garage. It was rumored that he lifted automobile engine blocks for exercise.

During the first week, Scott learned from Becky the details of working in a drive-in. Becky worked hard. When business was slow, she launched out on a project of cleaning the grill or washing the windows. But even when they were working side by side, she would seem to withdraw from him, her blue eyes reflecting unhappiness. Scott didn't say anything to her, and in a few minutes she'd return and they could talk again.

"Basically, what's wrong with me?" Scott asked one morning while they cleaned out the grease trays on the grill.

"Nothing."

"C'mon, Becky, be honest. I can take it. Is it my silver braces clash with the gold-rimmed glasses?"

"I've never noticed."

"I've got so much metal on my face I'm afraid to get too close to a TV set. I ruin the reception. Is it that I'm only 160 centimeters tall?"

"Centimeters?" she asked.

"I think I sound taller in the metric system. Do people make fun about my playing the oboe in orchestra?"

"No."

"The oboe hasn't really made it in the popular market. But someday I'm going to have a group that plays for dances that will have an electric oboe. I haven't figured out the details yet."

Becky never stopped working.

"Why can't I get a date?" he asked.

"Beats me," she answered. "Are you going to help me lift out this rack?"

"Sure." He bent down and slid out the grease-laden rack.

"Do you try to get dates?" she asked.

"I phoned Pam once."

"What'd she say?"

"Hello."

"That's all?" she asked.

"I'd rather not go into it. It's personal."

Everyday at noon Joe walked over from the garage to have lunch.

"C'mon out," he'd order Becky.

While Scott cooked Joe's hamburger, she'd sit for a few minutes with him. Joe spent his time complaining about his boss, the people who brought their cars into the garage, and her. Before he left, he'd say to Scott, "Put it on my tab," which meant Becky would pay for it.

During the second week Scott worked there, Joe got angry at Becky for some reason. They began to argue about something. Scott tried to listen but he had a line of little league players waiting for super dips. Finally Joe stood up, banged his fist on the table, and walked off. Becky watched him go, came inside, paid for Joe's meal, and helped Scott serve super dips. She remained quiet for the rest of the day.

After two days Joe came back. She hurried out to talk to him while he wolfed down a hamburger and fries. When she came back, she seemed happy.

A week later Scott asked her if she'd mind if he called her up at night to help him build his confidence.

"Becky, this is Scott."

"Hello, Scott."

"Hello, Becky," he said confidently. "You don't mind if I talk on the phone with you?"

"No, I don't mind. Joe's out at a party with some guys tonight."

"I just want to get practice talking. Nothing serious, you understand. Like the weather. How do you like the weather?"

"Fine."

"Me too. I've always liked weather," Scott added, and then after a long pause asked, "Becky, what do girls look for in a guy?"

"That's hard to say. It depends on the girl."

"Well, what do you like? Somebody who treats you rotten?" There was silence from the other end.

"He even swears in front of you, doesn't he?" Scott asked.

"You don't like him, do you?" she asked.

"What do I know? He's the success, not me. Maybe it's something I should try. Let's say you and I were going steady. I'd go to your home after work, sit down in front of the TV, drink Fresca, and watch the baseball game. Say something to me."

"How's the game?"

"Don't bother me when the White Sox are batting!" Scott roared into the phone. "Can't you let me have five minutes in peace?

"How'd I do?" Scott asked returning to his normal voice. "I really walked over you, didn't I? It's not as hard as I thought it'd be."

"I don't like it," Becky said, her voice straining.

"But that's what Joe does to you."

"Is it?" she asked.

"Sure. You're not very serious about him, are you? I mean, you'd never do a dumb thing like get married to him, would you?"

"I don't know. He's asked me."

"I think he'd probably treat you the same way after you were married. I'd never treat you that way, though, even if we were married."

"Oh? How would you treat me?"

"Special. Like if we were married and had two cars, I'd trade cars with you once a month and take yours in to have the oil changed. You'd never have to worry. And I'd empty the bag on the vacuum cleaner."

"I think we'd better hang up now," she said, her voice melancholy.

"Sure. I didn't say anything wrong, did I?"

"No. Goodbye."

"Yeah, I'll see you tomorrow."

When he went to work the next day, she worked quietly.

"You're not mad at me or anything are you?" he finally asked.

"No. Just thinking."

"I'm sorry if I said anything that hurt you.about you and Joe."

"It's okay. Maybe I needed to hear it."

"I think you're a fine person, Becky. Like the time you threw in four cents of your own money so that little kid could have enough for a cone.

"I think you're nice too."

"You, a girl, think that?" Scott asked, wiping off the counter. "I wish I were. I feel like the friendly neighborhood zero."

"You aren't."

"If I lettered in football, then I'd be somebody. I'd have a red R on my jacket. When I walked down the street, people would stop and say, 'Look, he's got a letter on his jacket.' Then I'd be somebody, and Pam would go out with me."

"You're somebody now. You just haven't realized it."

"If I was just better at talking to people. My dad talks to people all the time. Even gas station attendants. He just walks up and starts talking. By the time the tank's full, they're old friends."

"You can learn," she said. "Talk to the customers."

"Why not?" he answered.

A few minutes later a Volkswagen with three college girls from California stopped for burgers and fries and drinks. Becky cooked the burgers and fries while Scott got the drinks ready.

"Nice day, isn't it?" Scott leaned over the counter to talk to one of the girls.

"Yeah."

"Tell me, how're things in California? Are the oranges doing well?"

"What?" the startled girl asked, upset by the intense manner with which Scott spoke to her.

"The oranges in California. How're they doing?"

"I dunno."

Scott leaned farther out, straining to catch some threads of sanity in the conversation. "I guess if they weren't doing well, we'd have heard?"

Now almost shouting, Scott continued. "I mean, since we haven't heard, we can assume we'll have a good crop of oranges this year." Almost as a command, he barked out, "Wouldn't you say that?"

The girl backed away.

"I see you are driving a Vokswagen. How is the gas mileage?"

"I'm not sure."

"I think that's funny!" Scott yelled, his eyes open wide. "You got a small car so you'd get good gas mileage. And yet you don't even know what gas mileage you're getting. Don't you think that's funny? *Well, don't you?*" Scott barked, his voice cracking.

"Please, could we have our food?" one of the girls pleaded.

As soon as the food and money exchanged hands, the girls ran to the car and drove off, missing the driveway and going over the curb.

Scott and Becky watched them speed off. "Now you see what I mean. I never say the right thing. That's why I'm so afraid to call Pam. I'd mess the whole thing up."

"Look, if you want, Scott, I'll help you phone her after work."

After work they crossed the street to the bowling alley where there was a phone booth. Becky sat Scott down and calmly discussed with him how to make the phone call to Pam.

Then she led him to the phone booth. Halfway there, he stopped and practiced saying hello in lower and lower tones. "Hello, hello, hello, hello." A departing bowler stole a worried glance at him and then quickly hurried out the door.

Becky dialed the number and handed him the phone.

"Hello, hello, hello" he said finally reaching the desired pitch. "Pam, this is Scott. I'm your paper boy . . . Oh, I'm sorry about that. Tell your father I'll try not to throw it on the roof anymore. Goodbye.

"Maybe I'll call her a couple of times just to break the ice." Scott told Becky as they left. "Was my voice low enough?"

Joe had been waiting for Becky, his late model sports car parked at the drive-in. When he saw Becky and Scott coming out of the bowling alley, he hurried over to them.

"What were you two doing?" he asked suspiciously.

"We were making a phone call," Becky said.

Joe walked over to Scott, and stared at him angrily. Joe jabbed one finger at Scott's chest.

"Don't get ideas about spending time with Becky after work," he said sharply.

Glancing over to Becky, he ordered. "C'mon. I'm in a hurry."

A few days later Scott received the box containing an instruction book and record teaching karate, and an eight-by-ten glossy photograph of someone who claimed to be the king of karate.

That night Scott began his instruction. Over the next several days he spent hours looking in the full length mirror and shouting "Heaaah!" His parents grew to love and appreciate their backyard, spending much time there, as far away as they could get from the house.

"Becky, how come you sometimes don't come to church?" he asked one morning while they cleaned up the wrappers left from the night before.

"Some Sundays I'm with Joe at the beach or else at the car races. Why?"

"Your parents don't make you go?" he asked.

"My real parents are divorced. My stepfather isn't a member, and my mom doesn't want to make him mad. About the only time he's home is on Sunday."

They finished up outside and went in to make up some hamburger patties. "I thought it was going to be great at first when Mom remarried. The second week he took me and my sister out on Saturday. He took us to a fair and bought us cotton candy and hot dogs, took us on rides, and even bought us both a huge teddy bear. After he got us home, he quit paying any attention to us. It was as if his getting us the teddy bear proved what a loving stepdad he was. Now he doesn't talk to us except to yell. Sometimes I wish I could leave home."

"With Joe?"

"I don't know. Him or somebody else. I seem to attract guys like Joe."

Scott wiped his eyes and then continued to slice up some onions. "Becky, come with me Wednesday to church. Our Explorer post is having somebody come in to teach dancing. You'd have a good time. And you should see some of those guys. They're all taller than me, and some of them have their own cars."

"What about Joe?" she asked. "He gets very mad."

"You leave Joe to me," Scott said, looking at his karate-toughened, onion-juice-covered hand.

"What would I wear?" she asked.

"A dress if you have one."

"I do, but I don't wear dresses much because Joe never likes me to dress up. He says we're never going any place where we need to worry about how we look."

After work Scott and Becky walked over to phone Pam.

"What're you going to say?" Becky asked.

"Don't worry. You treat me like such a kid sometimes. I have it all figured out. A little light conversation to put her at ease. Then I just ask her if she'll go with me to the movies Saturday."

Becky got in the phone booth first, and he crowded in after her. With the door open they had more room in the booth, but the fan didn't run.

Becky dialed the number for him.

"Hello, is this Pamela Robertson who lives at 345 Riverside Drive? . . . Pam, this is Scott McCovick who lives at 349 Riverside Drive."

Scott cupped his hands over the phone and asked Becky, "Now what?"

"I told you we should've practiced," she whispered. "A little light conversation, remember?"

He stood looking at the phone as if he'd never seen one before.

"Say something!" Becky said.

"Pam," he continued, "I saw you spraying for dandelions a few days ago. What kind of weed killer do you use?"

Becky grimaced.

"No, that's okay," Scott added. "You don't need to go all the way out to the garage to find out. I'll ask your dad someday."

In order to start the fan running so they could get some air, Scott crowded into the booth and closed the door. Becky could just barely breathe.

"You sure did a great job. I bet you killed off every dandelion in your yard. That's what I like about you, Pam. You're thorough."

"I've got to get out of here," Becky whispered to Scott. He put the phone down, opened the door, and let her out. Then he grabbed the phone, and stepped inside the booth.

"Pam, are you still there? . . . No, nothing's wrong. Pam, I'm planning on going on a mission . . . Yes, in about three years . . . Well, that's kind of you to say. I just didn't want you to think I was out to get married right after high school."

"What are you doing?" Becky asked impatiently.

"I'm putting her at ease," Scott defended.

"Pam, what did you say? . . . Yes, I guess it does sound like I'm talking to somebody else at the same time. Well, keep it up with your lawn. Goodbye."

"You didn't ask her out," Becky said, trying to be kind.

"It didn't come up in the conversation. Give me time. Pam is a wonderful girl. She pays attention in seminary class. I know because I sit behind her and watch her all the time. What if she says no?"

"Why should she say no?"

"Why? Who wants to go out with an oboe player who is also the oldest paper boy in town?"

"So what if she does say no?"

"Don't say it. If she says no, it's all over between me and girls. I'll become an Olympic swimming champion."

The next day at work, Scott gave Becky a karate demonstration. Resting a board between two bricks, he brought his hand down swiftly and broke the board neatly in two.

"Scott, that's great!" Becky said.

"Well, it's a start," he said modestly.

"What do you mean? It's terrific!"

"Actually it's not impressive as it looks. I took a board and cut about two-thirds of the way through and then filled it up with plastic wood. I've got another board here to show off when those little league players show up."

During lunch Joe found out that Becky was going to activity night with Scott.

He walked up to the window and said, "Come out here."

"Your hamburger's almost ready," Scott answered.

"Stay away from my girl!" Joe yelled at him.

"I just asked her if she'd like to go to church with me tonight."

"She's not going anywhere with you or anybody else!" Turning around to Becky, he asked, "Are you?"

"You don't own me, Joe. I can go to church if I want to."

Joe whirled around to talk to Scott.

"You come out here, or I'm going to come in and get you."

"Yes, sir." On his way out, Scott spotted the board and the two bricks. He picked them up and carried them out, setting them up on the picnic table.

"Ahhhhmmm," Scott cleared his voice. "I should warn you," he said, his voice still too high, "that although I may appear to the casual observer to be harmless, I've been trained in the martial arts."

"Break your date with her," Joe demanded.

"Why? So you can yell at her and make her feel crummy. She deserves better treatment."

"I'm gonna break your head." Joe started walking toward Scott.

"If you hit me in the mouth, you're going to waste over a thousand dollars in dental care. There may be a law suit."

"You asked for it, kid."

"Wait, Joe. Don't do anything hasty. See this board. Heeaaah-" Scott's hand broke the board in two.

Joe stepped up to Scott and launched his right fist into Scott's mid-section, doubling him over. Joe turned and left.

Scott lay down on the ground, gasping for breath, while Becky knelt down and tried to comfort him.

The first words he was able to speak were, "I want my money back."

That night he met Becky at church. As she walked up to the door, one of the older guys in the post saw her and said, "Wow! Look at that! She's beautiful! Who's she gonna dance with?"

"That's my friend. I invited her tonight. Of course, I had to fight her former boyfriend first. Joe Kruglak."

"You fought Joe Kruglak?"

"Sure, I'll tell you about it sometime. But you'll excuse me now, won't you?" Scott made a grandiose gesture of opening the door for Becky.

Thursday after work, Scott and Becky again called Pam.

"Pam, this is Scott . . . You found out what weed killer you were using? . . . Yes, I'm sure it's very good. Pam, when do you get your braces off? . . . You know, we got braces about the same time and we're going to get them off about the same time. I mean, it's an experience we've shared, isn't it? When I first got them, I got part of an apple peeling caught in them. Maybe you remember. That was when I spent a couple of days with my hand in front of my mouth."

Becky closed her eyes and shook her head.

"No, Pam, Becky's just a friend. Why? . . . Oh, really? He is? Look, you tell him that Becky is a fine girl . . . No, I think she broke up with Joe. Look, to give you an idea of what kind of girl Becky is, I hope she won't mind me saying this. You know I work with her at the Dairy Dip. She is very good about cleaning the grease trays on the grill. Not just once a month, but at least once a week. You know what I mean? . . . Look, you tell Mike to come around tomorrow and I'll introduce him to her.''

Scott turned to Becky and gave her a smile.

"Pam, if you come with him, I'll let you have our 89 cent banana split for only 59 cents.''

Becky tapped him on the shoulder and shook her head, making a round 0 with her thumb and index finger.

"Pam, I'll even do better than that. I will buy you a banana split. Just for you, though, not for Mike. Okay? Bye.''

He hung up the phone and grinned at Becky.

"Pam's cousin is in the Explorer post at church, and he really likes you. He wants to take you to a fireside Sunday evening. You'll say yes, won't you? Because if you do, then I can ask Pam, and we can double, and Pam's cousin can use his dad's car.''

"Is he the tall one?'' Becky said with interest.

"None other.''

He walked Becky home, wheeling his bike.

"Poor girl,'' he finally muttered.

"What do you mean?'' Becky asked.

"Pam. She's really fallen for me.''

"How can you tell?''

"Well, maybe I shouldn't say this, but this morning when I was delivering papers, she was outside spraying for crabgrass.''

"So?'' Becky asked.

"So? You don't see what that means?''

"No.''

"Becky,'' Scott said, placing his hand on her arm, "You'd better stick with me for awhile. When it comes to things like this, you're such a child.''

The Emergence
of Butterflies

"The butterfly is the most beautiful and graceful of the insects. Butterflies fly from flower to flower drinking the sweet liquid called nectar. It is hard to believe that a beautiful butterfly was once a creature called a caterpillar." *(World Book Encyclopedia)*

Dan nervously checked his appearance in the hall mirror and then knocked on the door of Elizabeth's dorm apartment.

Inside the apartment, Elizabeth finished with her hair, stepped back to examine the effect, and told her roommate, "Well, it'll just have to do, won't it, because that's Dan now. Will you get the door? Tell him I'll be ready in a minute."

A short time later, her roommate came back. "Wow! Where did you find him?"

"We are both on a stake Young Adult committee."

"And you think he likes you?"

"Yes," Elizabeth smiled, "I think he does."

SUBJECT: Lisa (Elizabeth)

AGE: 13 years

EVENT: Discussion in the girl's locker room of junior high school

"Lisa," her friend Kara burst out excitedly, "I've talked to Ralph!"

"What did he say?" Lisa answered quickly, but then catching herself, she added cooly, "Not that I care."

"He said that you said that he said that he didn't like you, but he said that he didn't say that."

81

"He did so," Lisa accused. "He told Mike who told Janice who told Shelley who told me."

"He said that even if he did say it, which he didn't, he was joking. He said that he does like you."

"If he likes me," Lisa asked, putting a fresh stick of gum in her mouth, "then why did he throw an eraser at me yesterday?"

"Silly," Kara said knowingly, "that's how boys show they like a girl."

"It is?" Lisa asked.

"Sure. Larry Hill threw a water balloon at me last week, and I know he likes me."

"How do you know?"

"Because his face gets red when he talks to me."

"Oh," Lisa considered. "I wonder if Ralph's face would get red if I talked with him."

"I hope I'm not too late," Elizabeth said as she greeted Dan in the dorm living room.

"The way you look tonight," Dan said, standing up to greet her, "I'd wait a long time just to catch a glimpse." They walked to his car. "Have you ever heard of a restaurant called L'Epicure?"

"No."

"It's several miles from here, but it's nice. French cuisine. I'm afraid I picked up the taste for European cooking on my mission. Are you interested?"

"It sounds fun," she answered. "It also sounds like you're a connoisseur of good food."

SUBJECT: Dan

AGE: 16 years

EVENT: First prom date

The dance was over. Dan carefully maneuvered his dad's car out of the high school parking lot. "I thought we'd go out to eat," he said suavely.

"Great!" his date said. "Where?"

"Of course, because of the prom, many places will be full."

"How about the Pyrenes?" she suggested. "My parents go there."

"I'm sure it'll be full," Dan answered quickly.

"Okay, how about the Bonanza?"

"That will be full."

"McDonald's?" the girl pleaded.

"Full," Dan answered firmly. *"But don't worry. I know a place that's never full."*

"What's it called?" she asked suspiciously.

"Big Alice's Truck Stop Diner and Reloading Emporium. You get all the hashbrowns you can eat."

"Oh," the girl said with disappointment.

The old diner seemed to be leaning into the wind along the nearly deserted section of the old highway that had been abandoned with the construction of the interstate. Apparently a few truckers still went out of their way because two large semi-trucks were parked outside.

"My dad gave me ten dollars to take you out to dinner," Dan said as they pulled to a stop in front of the place, *"but, gosh, you could eat here for a week for ten dollars."*

Alice, a huge woman, stood behind the counter with her arms folded and argued politics with two truckers. Dan and his date moved quickly to the other end of the long row of stools along the counter and sat down. In a minute, Big Alice sauntered down to get their order. *"Whataya want?"*

"Two hamburgers with everything," Dan said, *"plenty of hashbrowns, and a couple of donuts for dessert."*

"Is it okay, what I ordered for you?" Dan asked his date. *"My dad said that the guy is supposed to order. It's etiquette."*

The two truckers and Big Alice continued their argument as she cooked their order.

"You can't say that!" one trucker argued.

"Well, I'm saying it!" the other trucker roared. *"The trouble with people today is that nobody wants to fight! Especially the kids today. They couldn't fight their way out of a paper bag!"*

Suddenly the three looked down the long row of empty stools to Dan and his date.

Dan nervously smiled at them.

In a few minutes, Big Alice brought their food and then left.

The girl carefully examined the hamburger. *"The meat's all greasy,"* she complained.

"That used to bother me, too, when I first started eating here," Dan eagerly explained, *"but I learned a little trick."* Grabbing some napkins, he picked up her hamburger patty and blotted it with the napkins. *"There,"* he said proudly, *"how's that?"*

He eagerly ate, but she took a fork and only probed the food with it.

"Aren't you even going to eat your hashbrowns?" he asked.

"They're greasy, too."

"Yea, but they're great with catsup." He picked up the catsup bottle, and in his eagerness, dumped the entire contents on her plate. Some of it splashed on her formal.

"Whoops," he said apologetically.

"Please," she said, beginning to cry, "take me home."

"Okay," Dan agreed. "Why don't you take a donut with you in case you get hungry on the way?"

As they drove to the restaurant, Dan turned on the radio for a minute to hear the score of the university football game. "Do you like football?" he asked.

"A little. I used to know a boy in high school who played. Were you on the football team in high school?"

"Yes," he smiled, "for two days."

SUBJECT: Dan

AGE: 16 years

EVENT: Football practice

"Report to my office when you're dressed," the coach growled to Dan in the locker room after the practice.

A short time later, Dan sheepishly stood in front of the coach's desk.

"I'm dropping you from the team," the coach rasped.

"Why? I take good care of my uniform. I keep all the training rules. Why drop me?"

"Because you can't play football!" the coach said harshly.

"Did you go steady with your friend who played football?" Dan asked Elizabeth.

"No. At one time he said he was interested in me, but we never got along very well."

SUBJECT: Lisa (Elizabeth)

AGE: 16 years

EVENT: A ride home with Larry Hill, local football hero

"Did you see Friday night's game?" Larry asked as he helped her into the car.

"Oh, sure. You were wonderful!"

"Thanks."

"I bet you have to practice hard to get so strong and fast. Just watching you run around the other team is so exciting."

"Things have always come easy for me. 'Natural talent' is the way the paper describes it."

"But you must train hard."

"No," he answered, *"training is for people who don't have natural talent."*

"Are you going to play in the pros?" she asked.

"Oh, sure," he answered confidently. *"I'm going to be a legend in my own time. Someday you'll see me on TV and you'll tell people that you knew the great Larry Hill and that he gave you a ride home from a school pep assembly practice."*

"Okay," she smiled, *"I'll do my part if you do yours."*

"It might be a nicer memory if you'd sit a little closer," he suggested. Turning on his four-track stereo to mood music, he casually put his arm over her shoulder. *"You know, Lisa, I was watching you tonight. I think I could really fall for you."*

She sat forward, leaving his arm dangling in the air. *"Larry, do you know where I live? It's on Fairmont."*

"Sure, I know."

"Then where are you driving?"

"I thought we could go up on the hill overlooking town and look at the moon . . . and talk."

"You can see the moon really well from my house," she suggested.

He looked at her suddenly with a puzzled expression. *"You're joking? You don't want to go up there with me?"*

"I've got to go home. My parents will be worrying."

He angrily flipped off the music, made a U-turn in the middle of the block, and sped back toward her house. *"I'll tell you one thing,"* he finally said, *"there are not many girls in our school who'd turn down attention from me."*

"Really? Maybe I'll be a legend in my own time too."

"You're making fun of me, aren't you?"

"Larry, you've got the whole world telling you how great you are. Isn't that enough?"

"Why won't you go up there with me and talk?"

"I'll talk with you in our kitchen over popcorn. Why do you want to go there?"

"I might want to kiss you."

"And parking up there has worked with other girls?"

"Look, who else ever pays any attention to you? I'm doing you a favor."

"You sound so sorry for me," she said. "Is a kiss from you such a prize?"

"Other girls think so," he answered crisply.

"Suppose I just let them have my share."

"But my cousin says that you are a good athlete," Elizabeth said to Dan.

"I play racquetball. I've been state champion three times. Since I wasn't cut out to be a football player, I substituted racquetball."

As he opened the car door for her outside the restaurant, she gave him a broad smile.

"Elizabeth, you have the most beautiful smile."

SUBJECT: Lisa
AGE: 16 years
EVENT: First day at school with braces

"How did it go at school today?" her mother asked as Lisa came in the house.

"Awful!" she complained. "One boy called me Metal Mouth. Another boy asked if he could use my mouth as an antenna for his radio. Kara said that at least it wouldn't cut down on my dating, since Larry has told everybody that I'm cold and conceited." She threw her books on the couch and ran to her room.

The hostess showed Dan and Elizabeth to a table. Dan helped her be seated.

SUBJECT: Dan
AGE: 17 years
EVENT: Laurel-Priest dating workshop

"Okay," the Laurel adviser coached Dan and a girl, "you've just entered the restaurant. Pretend that the card table is where the hostess wants you to sit. Show me how you sit down."

Dan sat down while the girl remained standing.

"Cut," the adviser said. "That's not right."

"What's wrong?" Dan asked.

"What about your date?"

"Oh, yeah," Dan agreed. "Hey, sit down; rest your feet," he said, pointing to the empty chair.

"No," the adviser corrected, "help her be seated."

"She can sit down by herself. I've seen her do it hundreds of times."

"You are a gentleman," the adviser said.

Wearily he stood up. "If you ask me, gentlemen go to plenty of extra work."

"Do it!" the adviser ordered.

"How?"

"Pull the chair out so she can sit down and then slide the chair in closer to the table."

"Not that much!" the girl cried as he pushed her into the edge of the table.

"Okay," the weary adviser continued, "now we come to ordering."

"Elizabeth, what would you like?"

"Everything looks good. Any suggestions?"

"May I suggest," he said with a flourish, "La Supreme de Chapon Montmorency?"

SUBJECT: Dan
AGE: 17 years
EVENT: Laurel-Priest dating workshop
"Now that you've ordered," the Laurel adviser continued, "it's time for some pleasant conversation."

"My sister had a nosebleed last night," Dan said. "We must've packed a box of tissues before we got it stopped."

"Cut!" the adviser shouted. Fighting to gain control, she quietly continued. "You don't discuss that at a dinner table."

"What am I supposed to say?" Dan asked.

"Find out more about her interests," the adviser said.

"Elizabeth, what are you majoring in?" Dan asked.

"Computer science."

"How did you ever decide on that?"

"To tell you the truth, I can't remember. I know that I liked math in high school."

SUBJECT: Lisa
AGE: 17 years
EVENT: Another dateless Friday night
"Lisa, can I come in?" her mother asked just outside her door. Lisa opened the bedroom door for her mother.

"Are you all right? You spend so much time in here all alone. We worry about you."

Lisa sat silently on the edge of her bed, and then suddenly blurted out, "Mom, am I so horrible? Other girls have dates. Why won't anybody ask me out? What's so terrible about me?

"I think you're terrific."

"Oh, Mom, you're supposed to think that. You're my mother."

Her mother sat down with her on the bed. "Lisa, did you know that boys develop slower in their interests in the opposite sex? In a while, some of the boys at church will get their heads out of a car engine, look around, and see what a beautiful woman you're becoming."

"Sure," Lisa complained, "and then they'll go on their missions, and I'll wait for another two years."

"Okay, you've got some time on your hands. Why not use it wisely? What talents and skills would you like to gain by the time you're grown?"

Lisa thought for a minute and then said, "I want to learn to play the guitar."

"Fine, you'll have time."

"I want to learn mathematics."

"Good. That will please your father."

"And I want to learn how to sew the way you do."

"Okay."

"I want to run on the girl's track team."

"That'd be exciting," her mother said, reaching out for Lisa's hand. "You can do all those things and more while you wait for the boys to mature."

"And what are you majoring in?" Elizabeth asked Dan.
"Business.

SUBJECT: Dan
AGE: 18 years
EVENT: Discussion with his boss
"Dan, how long have you worked here?" his boss asked one day.
"A year."
"It's time we changed you from stocking shelves and taught you how to sell clothes. Come with me." They walked up on the balcony and looked down at the activities on the first floor. "What do you think we sell here?"

"Men's clothes," Dan said.

"Oh no, we sell much more than that. Men come here because they need confidence to help them make a promotion in their company or to ask that special girl to marry them. We have the finest clothes in this city, and some of the most influential men in town shop here because they want the assurance that comes from quality tailoring."

"I never really thought about that before," Dan said, suddenly impressed with his boss.

"You're from Minnesota?" Dan asked over salad. "Is that where you went to high school?"

Elizabeth nodded. "Just outside Minneapolis."

"The great carefree happy days of high school," Dan said with a laugh. "Was it that way for you?"

"No, often it was painful."

SUBJECT: Lisa

AGE: 17 years

EVENT: Discussion with Kara in art class

"The face you're painting is so beautiful," Lisa said, admiring Kara's oil portrait.

"Thanks."

"But she looks a little lonely to me," Lisa remarked.

"Oh no, she's not lonely at all. With her looks, she's always got boys around her."

"I suppose so," Lisa replied. *"Still, there's something sad about her."*

"No, she's happy, just like me."

"Well, you certainly have boys around you; that's for sure."

"You could, too," Kara suggested.

"How?"

"Just be a little more like other girls. Being a genius in mathematics doesn't help your chances."

"I'm no genius. I just like it."

"Sometimes it's smart to play dumb around boys," Kara advised.

"Somewhere there's a boy who won't be put down just because I have goals to improve."

"Where is he?" Kara asked.

"I don't know." Lisa said glumly.

"He isn't here in this school. Boys are afraid of you here."

"I don't know where he is."

"Face it, he doesn't exist. Boys have to be superior. That's how I get along so well with Larry, our football hero. He needs me to feed his ego."

"It isn't honest to pretend that you're not smart."

"Maybe not, but it gets dates. There are plenty of girls who'd love to go out with the great Larry Hill. But he's all mine."

The class bell rang, and they put away their paintings.

"Kara, maybe you're seeing too much of Larry."

"Why do you say that?"

"Once I heard him talking about you with some other boys in the hall."

"Don't worry, I've got things under control. Say—let me ask Larry to get one of his friends to ask you out. There's a party Friday night."

Lisa thought for a moment and then said, "You know I'm a Mormon. Do you really think I'd fit in at one of your parties?"

"Do you always have to be so strict? Can't you ever have any fun?"

"We have fun, Kara. It's just a different kind of fun. Thanks for thinking of me, but I'd better not."

They talked about high school over dessert.

"I never did feel very comfortable around girls," Dan confided.

"And I was busy with my classes and other activities," Elizabeth recalled, "but socially it was like I was watching my friends make bad choices. Eventually their choices caught up with them."

SUBJECT: Lisa

AGE: 17 years

EVENT: Second conversation with Kara

"You've finished your painting," Lisa said, admiring the portrait of the girl. "It's beautiful."

"You were right about one thing," Kara agonized. "She is sad and lonely."

"Why?"

"She's found out that she's been used," Kara said.

"What's wrong, Kara?"

"I'm pregnant."

"Larry?"

"Yes."

"Is he going to marry you?"

"Oh no, not him. He doesn't want to be tied down," she said bitterly. *"He told me he feels responsible, and so he'll pay for an abortion."*

"Kara, you won't do that, will you?" Elizabeth pleaded.

"I don't know what to do," Kara said slowly. *"Could we go somewhere and talk?"*

They walked to a park near the high school and sat in the swings and talked.

"Lisa, do you remember when we were in grade school? We were such good friends, weren't we? We were just like sisters. How have we gotten so far apart?"

"I still love you as if you were my sister," Lisa said.

"I know, but now I'm so different from you. How have I come to the place I am now? I've thought about it lately."

"What did you decide?" Lisa asked.

"The only thing that has separated us is that I've always done what others told me everyone else was doing, but you never did any of those things. Why didn't you?"

"I'm a Mormon," Lisa said simply, *"and we have a prophet of God who gives us warning. I guess I've just listened to him."*

"I wish I could be like you, but now I feel so old. I'll never be young again, and I've got a decision to make. What should I do?"

"Don't let them kill your baby."

"It's not a baby yet, is it? It's just a growth. How can you be so sure that it wouldn't be better to just do it the way Larry wants? He calls it getting it fixed."

"Our prophet's warned us against abortion," Lisa said. *"Will you talk to my bishop? Maybe he can help you decide what to do."*

"Okay, I'll talk with him."

"Did your friends in high school learn from their bad choices?" Dan asked Elizabeth.

"I'm afraid not."

SUBJECT: Elizabeth
AGE: 20 years
EVENT: Meeting Kara at the airport
Elizabeth had taken the flight from Minneapolis to Salt Lake City on her return to college. She had walked slowly past the car

rental agency three times, carefully studying the features of the attractive girl at the counter. Finally she approached the girl.

"Excuse me, are you Kara?"

"Lisa?" the girl cried. "Is that you?"

They threw their arms around each other, both chattering excitedly.

"What are you doing here?" Elizabeth asked.

"I was transferred from our L.A. office six months ago. Look, I've got a break coming. Let's go to get something to eat so we can talk."

They sat at a small table and talked, filling each other in on their lives since they had last been together.

"I lost track of you after you left town," Elizabeth said. "My bishop said you never talked with him."

"Oh, I changed my mind and just had the problem fixed," Kara said lightly.

"Oh," Elizabeth said, trying not to betray her disappointment.

"I guess you're shocked, but it's quite common these days."

"But why did you suddenly leave town after that?" Elizabeth asked.

"I had to get away," Kara said, pursing her lips nervously, "and so I ran away."

"But where did you live? What did you do?"

Kara shook her head slowly. "You don't want to hear about that." She took a final drag on her cigarette and exhaled slowly. "But look, I'm all squared away now. I'm into group therapy, and it's really helped me get rid of all my guilt feelings about everything. What a relief not to feel guilty about anything! But I guess you know about that, because you've never done anything to feel guilty about."

A few minutes later, Elizabeth asked, "What happened to Larry Hill?"

"Last I heard he was working as a DJ in a disco in California."

"I guess that makes him one of the real men, doesn't it?" Elizabeth said. "He always needed that assurance."

"I've heard he's still running around just like he did in high school," Kara added. "I guess I am, too, for that matter. I'm just not ready to settle down."

Dan paid the check and took Elizabeth's arm as they left the restaurant. "Lisa, we can go to the movies like we planned, but there's something else I'd rather do."

"What's that?"

"Take me to your computer," he said with a metallic ring to his voice.

The remote computer terminal on campus looked more like a typewriter than a computer. Dan sat beside her as she turned it on.

"How do you address a computer?" he asked. "Hi, big fella?"

"That would work if it were programmed for that. For this one, a simple combination of numbers and letters will do."

"Sounds sinister," he said.

As she enthusiastically tried to teach him some computer games, he found himself just smiling, nodding his head, delighting in watching the features of her face.

"You really like this, don't you?" he asked as they left the building.

"I really do. And your male ego isn't threatened by a girl who enjoys computers?"

"No. Someday when I have a chain of stores all over the West, maybe I can get you to show me how to use a computer in business."

"It's a deal," she answered. "Now, sir, it's my turn. I want to learn how to play racquetball."

"Now? The way we're dressed?"

"Just show me where you play and explain the rules. Okay?"

Finding an empty court, they took off their shoes and entered the room. He explained the rules and strategy to her.

"Okay? I'll serve." Standing between the two painted lines in the room, he served an imaginary ball. In graceful slow motion, she returned his serve.

"Where'd it go?" he asked.

"It bounced off the wall an inch from the floor."

"Wow!" he laughed. "Nice return."

They played with the imaginary ball until they both collapsed side by side in laughter.

"Elizabeth, you know what?" Dan said while they were still sitting on the floor. "I feel terrific, just being with you. Everything is so natural. I don't have to prove anything with you. I feel that I could tell you anything about my hopes and dreams, and even some of the dumb things I do, and you wouldn't reject me."

"I know. I feel the same way."

"Let me tell you some deep secrets," he said with a grin. "I love apples, and I use the ash tray of my car to store my apple cores."

"I can take that," she smiled. "Here's one for you. About once a year I buy a can of pitted black olives, go in my room, put an olive on each finger, and pop them one by one in my mouth."

"Here's one," he said. "Once I was asked not to sing in a youth conference chorus. You know, they always say we don't care whether or not you can sing. Well, I volunteered and was told to just move my lips."

"I know how to change the oil in a car," she confessed.

"One of the most successful elders in our mission was Elder Reed. Once at a zone conference I got a chance to meet him. I really was excited. I walked up to him, stuck out my hand, and said, 'Hi there, I'm Elder Reed.' He looked at me strangely. I realized my mistake and then said, 'No, wait. You're Elder Reed.' He looked at me like I was crazy and walked away."

"I love to waltz," she said.

"Teach me. Now."

"Here?" she said, looking around at the empty racquetball court.

They waltzed in stocking feet to her songs and his regimental one, two, three, one, two, three.

On the way out, they decided to walk through the tunnel connecting the two buildings used for athletics.

"Have you ever heard the legend of this tunnel?" he kidded as they walked down the long hall. "When a couple who are going to become very good friends walks down this hall, legend says they hear an echo."

"Really?" she giggled.

"Dan and Elizabeth are falling in like!" he yelled. An echo returned his voice. "See that?" he asked. "It's the legend of the tunnel."

"Falling in like?" she asked.

"Sure, it's one step before falling in love."

They ambled down the long hall, holding hands, talking happily, the echoes of their voices, and their past, returning again and again back to them.

The Flowers
of Early Summer

She was young and beautiful—young enough to be largely unaware of the grace that unfolded with bashful uncertainty as the days passed. But in the third month of her 17th year, she died, cut down by a rare disease.

He was 18 and her friend. They never really dated. He had kissed her once at her 16th birthday party in front of her mother and everybody. He had done it as a joke, so that no one could accuse her of being "sweet 16 and never been kissed." But she had always seemed too young for him to consider her seriously.

They both lived in a small town in Montana. To the east was prairie, and to the west a range of mountains.

Because of the few LDS students in the high school, Dave and Cathy attended early morning seminary. Each morning at 5:00, he jabbed at the buzzing alarm clock, struggled out of bed, showered, dressed, ate a hurried breakfast, and drove to her home to pick her up. She often kept him waiting, but finally she would rush out—a book, a purse, a piece of toast in one hand, a hair brush and a coat in the other.

One evening in April, her mother phoned Dave to say, "Cathy won't be going to school tomorrow, so you won't need to pick her up for seminary. She isn't feeling well."

That was the beginning.

Dave graduated from high school in May, was ordained an elder in June, and began working in a clothing store in order to earn money for his mission. Each day after work he visited her. On the days when she was feeling better, he found her in the backyard.

Her backyard had once been mostly lawn. But through the years the vegetable garden had been enlarged until now there was left only a small strip of lawn in front of the patio. Even with the threat of losing all the lawn to the needed vegetable, her mother always insisted that a patch of flowers be preserved.

One day when he came, Cathy was lying on the lawn, her chin propped up by her two hands, intently studying the determined efforts of several bees that were working the flower garden. Dave paused at the gate and quietly watched her. She wore a pair of levis and a western-style shirt. Since he had visited her last, her long hair had been cut into a more practical summer style.

When he finally went through the gate, she turned and sat up.

"I wish I could spend all day watching flowers grow," he teased.

She stood up and came over.

"Who cut your hair?" he asked.

"My mother. Do you like it?"

"I like it fine."

They walked together, inspecting the long straight rows of beets, lettuce, and tomatoes.

"Did you have a date last night?" she asked.

"Yes, with Karen. We played miniature golf."

"Do you like her?"

"I don't know. She's okay. It's hard to get involved with anyone when I know I'm going on a mission in four months. Maybe she'll write to me."

He picked a small flower for her from a bush that clung to the trellis by the house.

"Will you write to me?"

"What do you want, a fan club? 'Dear Elder Dave, you are so great! All us girls at home are just sighing our lives away until you return.' Is that right?"

"It'll do," he grinned. "And I'll write each of you a mimeographed letter. 'Dear Sister Friend, We baptized 500 last week. I'm trying to remain the humble self that you've all grown to love. I hope that none of you are dating while I'm away.' "

"Is that the way it's going to be?" she asked.

"I guess not," Dave replied.

"Dave," she said, suddenly serious. "You will be a good missionary, won't you? You'll remember the Savior and represent him properly?"

"I hope so," he answered.

They sat on the lawn chairs on the patio.

"I was sitting here this morning," she said, "looking at the flowers in the garden. I remembered what the Savior said: 'Consider the lilies of the field, how they grow.' Where's that found in the Bible?"

"I thought I was finished with scripture chasing when I graduated from seminary," he teased.

"Okay, I won't press you. Anyway, that's not my question. I had a picture in my mind while I was thinking. I want to tell you about it."

She held the flower he had given her in both hands and studied it carefully.

"It's early morning," she began. "There are mists still hanging over the Sea of Galilee. A lone man walks along a path leading away from a small fishing village. It's the Savior. He walks up the slope away from the water. As he walks, he comes upon a patch of wild flowers. He kneels down to get a closer look. He reaches out and touches the petals. He bends over to examine the insides of the blossom. My question is, what does he see?"

"A flower."

"Is that all? Just a flower?"

"What else could he see?"

"Jesus was given the responsibility by Heavenly Father to create this earth. At one time, he knew the purpose of every feature of that flower. Did he remember all of those details? Or did his great mind understand the function of each part of the flower just by careful observation? That's my question."

"I can't answer that."

"I know, neither can I. But I don't believe that he ever considered anything to be common. I think he valued the beauty of every sunset, each view of the Sea of Galilee—in sunshine or in rain. I believe that he was sensitive to beauty. When he said, 'Consider the lilies of the field, how they grow,' I believe that he had considered those lilies in greater detail than most of us ever will."

Her father, home from work, came through the gate and began to pull some weeds from the garden. He was a quiet man who took pride in straight, neat rows of vegetables. Often when he worked, he whistled a tune with no recognizable melody.

He picked half a dozen strawberries, washed them off with the hose, and brought them over for Dave and Cathy to sample.

"They're coming along nicely aren't they?" he asked.

In June Cathy spent a week out of town undergoing tests at a university medical center. When she returned, she didn't look any better, and her parents were strangely evasive when asked what the specialists had found.

As the summer passed, Dave could see that she was slowly getting worse. Often when he came, she was in bed. Sometimes he only stayed a minute because she looked tired. But she enjoyed seeing him, and some days she felt good enough to talk.

"Dave," she said on one of his visits, "I found a scripture for your mission." She reached for the triple combination on the table by her bed, and, finding the place, read aloud: " 'Therefore, O ye that embark in the service of your God, see that ye serve him with all your heart, might, mind and strength, that ye may stand blameless before God at the last day.' *(D&C 4:2)* How's that?" she asked.

"You're determined to make me a good missionary, aren't you?" he asked.

"There's so much to be done. I wish I were going to be around to help."

He looked up, trying to read her face.

"I know what's happening. I'm dying."

"No, you're not."

"We traveled a thousand miles to see a team of doctors. After two days, we came home. My parents never say anything about the results. They won't talk about it. Now my dad asked me about taking a vacation to California. He wants to cash in his life insurance to get the money so we can all fly down. We've never gone on a big vacation like that before. When my parents come into my room, they're both so cheerful. But yesterday I heard my mother in her room crying. And the worst part is that we can't talk about it. We spend 20 minutes talking about the weather, clinging to the topic as if it were a life raft."

Just then her mother came in the room with another vase of flowers. Cathy's bedroom was filled with potted plants and cut flowers given to her by friends. Her mother picked up two vases of old flowers and left the room.

Cathy continued, "Dave, I need you to talk to. I can't talk to my parents yet. I need to tell someone how I feel so I can define it in my mind and see the limits of my fear and measure it. There must be boundaries to it."

They talked for a long time. Mainly he listened as she tried to find out if she could face her future.

"I know that none of us can be guaranteed a long life and that Heavenly Father won't deny me any blessings. But I don't want to leave this earth. I like it here."

Before he left, she asked, "Will you give me a priesthood blessing?"

"Shouldn't your dad do that?"

"He's already administered to me. I need a priesthood blessing so that I can face it and so that my parents and I can talk."

"I can have the bishop come over," he said weakly.

"No, you've got all the priesthood you need. I want you to give me a blessing."

"I've never given a priesthood blessing."

"It doesn't need to be today," she said.

"Do you mind if I talk to your dad and the bishop about it? If they approve, I'll be glad to."

Sunday afternoon he arrived prepared. He had spent two days in reading. He had talked to Cathy's father and the bishop and asked for their help and counsel. They had encouraged him to respond to Cathy's special request. He had fasted and prayed since Saturday morning.

When he came, she was waiting for him, sitting in a chair in her bedroom.

He stood behind her. The room was silent except for the out-door sounds coming through the open window. He placed his hands lightly on her head, touching the silky texture of her hair. Closing his eyes, he paused and then began, "Catherine Edmonds, by the power of the Melchizedek Priesthood which I hold, I place my hands on your head to give you a priesthood blessing. . ." The words seemed to flow easily and naturally. He blessed her that she would be comforted and that she would be able to talk openly to her parents about her condition.

When it was over, they both felt peaceful. He helped her into bed, sat down in the chair, held her hand, and talked with her until she fell asleep.

Monday afternoon when he came again, she was lying outside in a recliner. Her father was building a screened-in room with a covered roof so that she could spend more time outside.

"Daddy," she asked, "could we move those potted plants from my room out here? I'd like them planted in the garden with the other flowers."

"I don't see why not," her father answered. "Are you getting tired of them in your room?"

"No, I just want them to be here in the sun."

The next day when Dave arrived, her plants had already been transferred to the garden.

"Don't they look good?" she asked him. "I've been watching them all day. The bees have been visiting them. Out here they have the sun and the warm soil. I'm glad they're out here. Look at all they'd miss if they were still cooped up in the house."

Saturday he worked in the morning, but he took the afternoon off so he could be with her. They sat together in the enclosed patio.

In the late afternoon, dark clouds, which had been building to the west of them all day, finally moved in.

Her father gently asked, "Don't you want to come inside? It looks like rain."

"No, I like it out here. Let me watch the rain."

The summer storm struck with fury. The large drops were driven almost sideways by the wind.

Then the hail came. At first it was just one or two scattered, marble-sized stones striking the grass and bouncing back. But as the storm approached, the crashing of the hail on the green fiberglass roof of the patio sounded like hundreds of cannon rounds.

In a few minutes it was over. The lawn was covered with a layer of white.

Her father stood up and walked out into the garden. Standing in the light rain, he silently observed the damage. He picked up a broken stem from a tomato plant, examined it, and then let it drop back to the ground. He slowly made his way to the flower garden. The flowers had been flattened to the ground.

"Maybe we shouldn't have moved these plants out here," he said. "They would have been safe inside."

She stood up and, with some difficulty, went to her father.

"No, Daddy. I wanted them here in the garden. They were safe inside, but out here, even though it was only for a few days, they've had the warm sun and the bees and the gentle summer wind at night. I'm not sorry we brought them here. It was worth the chance just to have them in the garden—even for a short time."

Somehow they both realized that now they were talking about more than flowers. He held his daughter close to him while she repeated softly, "Daddy, it's going to be all right."

The next day she told Dave that she and her parents had finally talked about the future.

Two weeks later she was admitted to the hospital.

Three weeks later she died.

Some who attended the funeral may have wondered why, instead of the customary wreath of flowers on the casket, the family placed there a bouquet of flowers from their garden—flowers that had endured the hail and yet lived on.

Charly

"Roberts, we've got you surrounded, so don't try anything. We think the whole structure may be weakened. So just sit still until we can get both of you out safely. You've got a charge of kidnapping against you, but things will go easier for you if the girl gets down safely."

The policeman handed the portable megaphone to Charly's mother. "Charly, this is your mother. Don't worry. The police are doing everything possible to get you down. Just don't panic . . ." She broke down and began to sob. Charly, her long, wheat-blond hair waving as the car of the stalled Ferris wheel rocked gently in the wind, grabbed my hand and smiled. "Roberts, I hope you let this be a lesson to you. You can't hi-jack a Ferris wheel to Cuba."

It started innocently enough a year ago in May. Dad and I had jogged our two miles in the morning, and we were eating our nutlike cereal on the patio overlooking the city.

"Sam, you know the new manager I was telling you about?" Dad said as he took a vitamin pill and downed it with the rest of his orange juice. "Transferred here from Boston. He's finally found a house, and his family moved out here last week. He has a daughter Charlene about your age. Naturally, she doesn't know anybody here."

He paused, hoping I would volunteer and not force him to spell it out. "I was wondering if you'd take her out once just as a favor."

"Well, I'd like to but I'm kind of low on money right now. They don't pay much in the basement," I said, referring to his office on the eighth floor and my summer job as a shipping clerk in the basement of one of the large buildings in the city.

"Maybe I could help you out," Dad said. I was enjoying this.

"I won't need much. I'll take her to the museum, and then to the visitor's center, and then to the drug store for a milk shake."

"Why don't you take her to the country club for dinner?"

"Okay. I'll even get my jeep washed. I sure wish I could get it out of four-wheel drive."

"Okay. You win; take my car."

"That's a good idea. Thanks, Dad."

A few days later I made my way to her home. It was an ornate building, a little north of the capitol. I spent about ten minutes talking with her parents about the difference in humidity between Boston and Utah. Then finally she came down the stairs.

She was almost as tall as I, with a face that didn't need make-up. She was skinny and looked like a model for a diet soft drink.

I stood up, remembering a Cary Grant movie I saw once on TV. "Charlene, it is indeed a pleasure."

"The pleasure is mine," she said. As we shook hands she, still smiling, dug her finger nails into my palm.

We drove silently down the interstate to the country club.

"How much did your dad pay you for taking me out?" she asked.

"I was happy to ask you out." I exaggerated.

"What would you think about turning off the air conditioning? It's freezing in here."

"Why don't you check the blower so it's not aimed directly at you? It's very seldom I get to drive a car with air conditioning."

She sat and glared at the dashboard.

"Tell me, Charlene, how do you find the difference in humidity here as compared to Boston?"

"Don't call me Charlene."

"What then?"

"Charly."

She opened the side window and deliberately adjusted it so the hot air outside was blowing directly at me.

"It's wasting gas to have the air conditioner on and the window open," I said.

"You never told me how much your dad is paying you to take me out."

"Not enough, I think."

She folded her arms, turning away from me. The periodic brightness as we passed lamp posts showed tears on her face.

"I didn't mean that. Look, I'm turning off the air conditioner. There's a Kleenex in the glove compartment."

"Why would I want one?" she asked.

"Because you're crying."

"I'm not crying. My contacts are bothering me."

"Well, whatever," I replied. "The Kleenex is still in the jockey box."

"I've got my own," she said, rummaging through an old leather bag. Eventually she found one crumpled tissue that she smoothed out and used. "Will you take me home please?"

We rode in silence back to her home. I shut off the motor at her curb. "I'm sorry things didn't work out."

"It's no big thing."

"I did my best to make it a night you'd enjoy."

"Implying that I didn't do my best?"

"No, you probably did the best you could," I answered.

"I'd better go now. It's getting late," she said.

"It's only nine o'clock."

"Time really flies when I'm with you. I thought it was eleven."

"You think it's easy going out with a girl from Boston? My dad and I thought you'd like the country club."

"Listening to you talk about humidity and watching old golfers slap each other on the back?"

"Well it's not my idea of fun either," I said.

"No?" We stopped halfway up the walk.

"No."

We walked back to the curb, sat down and talked about things we always wanted to do but could never find anyone else do do them with.

A few minutes later we got back in the car, drove to a park, and bought 30 dollars worth of tickets for the Ferris wheel.

"What's your name?" Charly asked the attendant as he helped her into the Ferris wheel car.

"Raferty."

"Mr. Raferty, I'd like you to meet my fiance. He's just proposed, and you're the first one we've told."

"It's not true," I said. "I've just met her."

Mr. Raferty was hard of hearing. "Congratulations, kids."

"Thank you," Charly smiled. "Sam and I want to ride on your Ferris wheel for a long time. You understand, don't you?"

"Sure, I'm not that old," he said as I gave him several tickets.

We rode and talked. Up over the trees, the laughing children, the crying children, the picnicking families, the merry-go-round, and then back to earth and Mr. Raferty, who gave us a wink as often as he could.

"Sam, alias Utah Kid, maybe we're going to be friends."

I took her to church that next Sunday. The following Wednesday she began the missionary lessons. She began to jog with Dad and me in the mornings.

About three weeks later I took her fishing with me at Strawberry Reservoir. We left about four in the morning. When we got there, we rented a boat, rowed out to my favorite spot, and threw out the anchors. I baited the hooks with cheese and marshmallows and tossed my line out.

She curled up and went to sleep.

When she woke up, I had caught four nice trout, the sun had come and driven off the patches of fog, and ten other boats were anchored near us.

She studied the people in the boats around us. They were sitting quietly, watching their lines.

Suddenly she stood up, cleared her throat, and addressed the boaters with a Kissinger-like accent. "I suppose you know why we have asked you here this morning. We'll dispense with the minutes and move right along."

The people in the boats looked at her with disbelief.

"Because some of you have been putting marshmallows on your hooks, the Fish and Game Department has asked me to speak today. Clinical reports indicate that the fish in this lake have 53 percent more cavities. Do you know what this means?" she asked.

She waited. Most of the other boaters tried to ignore her. But that was hard to do.

"It means that the state of Utah *now* must stand the expense of sending a trout through dental school."

"Charly?" I asked.

"Yes, Utah," she said meekly.

"Normally we don't talk between boats. Please sit down."

I baited her hook and tossed it out. In a few minutes her line began to feed out steadily. I could tell it was going to be big when she set the hook. She followed my directions, and soon I dipped the net into the water, bringing up a four-pound rainbow.

After the fish had been taken care of, she stood up again and addressed the other boaters. "Do you people wish to know how I caught this fish? I used peanut butter on my hook. It sticks very well, its nutritious, and it does not cause cavities."

I pulled in the anchors and began to row out farther.

"We recommend creamy instead of chunky!" she shouted as a parting shot.

"Sam, where are we going?"

"Away."

"Is the fishing better where we're going?"

"No."

"I embarrassed you; is that it? Go ahead and say it."

"You embarrassed me." I splashed a little water on her so she wouldn't think I was mad.

"You've got no sense of humor, Utah. Life is for laughing."

I stopped rowing and threw out the anchors again.

"Sam, how many of those people in the boats do you think were Mormons?"

"Maybe half."

"A school of Mormons," she said.

I baited the hooks again and tossed the lines out. "Charly, you haven't said much about the Church to me, except 'Very interesting.' "

"Very interesting," she mocked. "I wanted to be fair, Sam. We New Englanders are noted for our fairness."

"Yes, I've read about the Salem witch trials," I countered.

"Very good, Sam. Stick with me and I'll make you a wit." She opened a sack of oranges and threw me one. "Okay, Sam, I guess I'm ready."

For a few minutes she concentrated on peeling her orange, her face strangely solemn. "Utah, I've read the Book of Mormon."

"What do you think about it?"

For a long time, she just looked out over the lake. And then in a quiet voice she began, "Humor them along, I said. Take the lessons; go to church. It's all just part of the tour after all. And then walk away laughing.

"I grew up in Cambridge, Sam. Our next door neighbor wrote a best seller on economics. My mother played bridge with the wife of a man who became one of Kennedy's advisers. We had as a weekend guest a man who later received a Nobel Prize. Do you understand what I'm saying?"

"What are you saying?" I asked.

"I've been exposed to the finest intellectual environment. Then you come to me with your 2½ minute talks. Why not three minutes for crying out loud? I thought I'd spend my life laughing at the world. There was so much to ridicule, so many balloons to pop. It would take a lifetime."

"Don't give me a dissertation, Charly. What about the Book of Mormon?"

"It's true," she answered simply. "I believe every word. The plates, the angels—all of it. Now I'm afraid of what that implies."

"Why?"

"When fall comes and I go back to school, and my friends come up giving the cynical smile and asking, 'Well, did the Mormons get you?' what do I say?"

"Tell them."

"They'll think I'm a fool."

"What are you interested in, truth or pretense?"

"You ask me that? That's the same question I've been using as a weapon against the world."

It was too late to be fishing, and the wind was starting to come up. I pulled in the anchor and started rowing for shore.

A week later she was baptized. She was beautiful in white. Her parents didn't come to the baptism.

"Are you going to ask me to marry you, Sam?" she asked while putting suntan lotion on my shoulders as we soaked in the sun one Saturday at the country club pool.

"You're not supposed to ask that."

"Male chauvinist. Why can't I ask it? Are you?"

"I don't know."

"Don't be so insistent, Sam. You've got to give me time. I'll have to think it over and let you know. So don't rush me, okay?"

I ignored her and lay back down on the warm sun deck.

"Sam, are you awake? You're going to get a sunburn."

"I'm awake," I answered sluggishly.

"Sam, I've thought it over. I accept. You're a lucky man."

I sat up and put a towel on my sore shoulders.

She leaned over like she was going to kiss me, but instead slapped me on my sunburn. "Race you to the diving board!"

She beat me there. We took turns diving. She was very good. While we were waiting our turn, she punched me on the chin in slow motion. "Sam, you son of a gun, asking me to marry you when we've only known each other part of a summer. You've got some nerve, Utah."

She stood on the board and did a perfect swan dive. I just dived off.

"Why the joke about marriage?" I asked.

"Who said I'm joking?"

She stood up at the board again. She addressed the line of swimmers waiting to dive. "For this next dive, I must have silence so that I may concentrate," she announced dramatically with a slightly European accent. "This dive is one that my family has passed down from generation to generation. If you will be quiet, then I will do it for you today."

A hush fell over the swimmers. She surveyed the pool. A waiter carrying food to a lounging couple stopped to wait. "So, I will do it." She slowly approached the middle of the board, stopped, put her arms out, seeming to be reaching for psychological strength. Then, summoning courage, she raced to the edge of the board, jumped in the air, tucked in her knees, and did a cannonball.

Two or three times a week we went back to the Ferris wheel.

Near the end of August we were walking around a shopping center on a Saturday afternoon. We were in a large discount department store. We passed the maternity clothes.

"How many children do you want, Sam?"

"At least six."

"So many? How come? Religious reasons?"

"That's right."

"Six kids. That's a bunch."

"They come one at a time. That way you can make all your mistakes on the first one."

"Careful, fella, I was the first one," she warned.

A while later we walked by the toy department and a row of dolls. She picked up six, but one fell down. "I can't get six, Sam." She put all but one of the dolls back. "I'll be a good mother, Sam. When I was little I had a doll and she was no problem at all. I just said, 'Go to bed and sleep,' and she did. So six will be nothing."

"You know, Charly, I've never really asked you to marry me."

"I noticed that. Yes, sir, I have noticed that."

We got what she needed, but on the way out I remembered I needed to get a coupling for our water hose. Since she was not really interested, we agreed to separate and then meet later. She suggested the jewelry counter.

I found the hardware section, found the coupling, and went back to the jewelry counter. She wasn't there. I waited for five minutes and then started walking around to see if I could find her.

After 15 minutes of looking, I heard a strangely familiar voice over the P.A. system. "Sam, Sammy, you hear me? This is Mommy. The nice men let me talk to you on the big radio. Sammy wherever you are in this big store, stop and listen to Mommy."

I looked around to see if anyone was looking at me.

"Sammy, if you can hear me, listen carefully. Remember when Mommy bought you a big bag of popcorn last week. Sam, go to the popcorn machine, and Mommy will be there. Do you understand? The popcorn place. Mommy will get you a big bag of popcorn. Mommy loves you, Sam."

A man standing next to me grabbed a handkerchief and blew his nose. "Poor little guy," he muttered to himself.

I walked over to the popcorn machine. There was Charly with a bag of popcorn in her hand.

I grabbed her arm and quickly escorted her out of the store.

"Sam, do you want some popcorn?" she asked. "You're mad at me, aren't you?"

"Get in the car."

"I was a bad girl."

"Why don't you grow up, Charly? You think the world was made for your amusement?"

"Don't preach to me, Sam. I'm sorry. Okay?"

I should have waited until I got control before I said anything, but I didn't.

She didn't defend herself but just sat there, holding that ridiculous bag of popcorn in her lap.

Then I said the thing that I shouldn't have. "You've been talking about marriage. Well, I'm not ready for marriage and especially not to someone who hasn't grown up yet." I drove her home, and she opened the door by herself and ran up the walk alone to the door.

I sat and watched her go.

I suppose I figured I'd let her stew for a couple of days and then call her up and tell her she was forgiven. But on Monday when I called, her mother said that she'd decided to go back to Massachusetts early for school. She'd left that morning. Her mother told me that Charly didn't want me to know where she was going, didn't want me to write or call, and didn't want to see me again.

After a week of long distance phone calls I was finally able to get her address. When I phoned, she hung up. I wrote to her several times. But she never answered. One day I got a large envelope with all my letters inside. None of them had been opened.

Then I quit my job and went back to school.

I tried to get in touch with her during Christmas vacation, but her parents went back to see her so she wasn't in town.

In June I was back in town. My dad got me a job on the first floor of the same building, in line with additional schooling, I guess.

One day at work I got a phone call from my dad who now was on the ninth floor. "She's back in town with a boy named Mark. I thought you might want to know."

That night I drove by her house. There was a small sports car with Massachusetts license plates parked in the driveway. I drove around her block about 20 times trying to formulate a plan. Nothing came to mind, so I finally just parked and walked up to the door.

They were in the backyard. The door was open and I went in. I could see Charly through the kitchen window, standing next to a Harvard type gesturing with a pipe in one hand.

"I'll be back in a minute. I'm going to change." Charly left him, walked into the kitchen, and into the hall.

She saw me and stopped. "Sam?"

"Hi, Charly."

"Are you real? For a minute there I thought you were the ghost of boyfriends past."

"My dad told me you were back. They say it's serious when she brings the guy home to meet the parents. Are you engaged?"

"I could be."

"Do you love him?"

"You're not supposed to ask that."

"Oh, I'm sorry."

"Would you like to meet Mark? He'd discovered a lot of investment opportunities right here in Utah. Maybe you two could work out a partnership."

"No, I'd better go." I started for the door.

Charly walked out with me. "Whatever happened to all those tickets we got for the Ferris wheel?"

"I still have them."

"I thought you'd use them for your other dates."

"No one else would understand."

"Oh."

We walked out to the jeep. "Did you ever get this thing out of four-wheel drive?" Charly asked.

"Sort of. Now I can't get it into four-wheel drive." We both smiled faintly.

"Why didn't you answer my letters?" I asked.

"I guess I felt like I'd made a fool of myself and didn't want to be reminded."

I walked over to the righthand side of the jeep, opened the glove compartment, and pulled out several faded, bent tickets.

"There are still a few left," I said, walking back to her.

"I wonder if they're still good," she said. Then, so I wouldn't misunderstand, she quickly added, "I mean you should find someone else to use them with."

"It wouldn't be the same. I'll just get rid of them," I said, ripping one of them up, letting the pieces flutter to the ground.

"Don't," she said, grabbing the others.

Our eyes met.

"Charly, couldn't we go somewhere and talk? Just to make sure things are the way we want them.

"I can't. It's too late."

"Maybe there's nothing left between us, Charly. I don't know. But I don't want to spend the rest of my life wondering what would have happened *if*. If there's nothing left, give me the piece of mind of knowing that."

"What do I tell Mark?"

"Just leave a note saying you're going for a ride, and you'll explain when you get back."

She went in the house and in a minute was back again.

We drove to the park, gave Mr. Raferty the rest of the tickets, and got in the Ferris wheel car.

"I was listening to Mark while I wrote the note. I think he just sold my dad an apartment building in Newton."

"Then the trip out here won't be a complete waste," I said.

"Mark will someday be governor of Massachusetts. I'm sure of it."

"He has a Word of Wisdom problem."

"You're always classifying people, aren't you? Do all Mormons do that?"

"You're a Mormon, remember?"

"You won't believe this, but I *have* been going to Church. And I have asked Mark about taking the lessons. He thought that was very funny."

"Are you in love with him?"

"I don't know. I have a high regard for him."

"That sounds pretty weak to me. You could say that about your milkman."

"Don't push me, Sam."

"I'm just asking you to wait before you do anything dumb like getting engaged to him."

"Why?"

"Well, for starters, he can't take you to the temple. A marriage with him would have a built-in divorce clause. And I can't forget you. Maybe at first you loved me more than I loved you. But I've had a year to catch up. Give me a chance."

She started going through her old leather bag. "You never can find anything when you need it. I put Kleenex in here, and it's there for months, but the minute I want it, it's gone."

"I have a clean handkerchief," I volunteered.

She took it, and wiped her eyes. "My mother ordered a cake for a garden party we are going to have tomorrow for Mark. She knows I haven't said yes to Mark yet, but the cake looks a lot like a wedding cake. She's trying to talk me into making an announcement at the party. You know, she isn't really that fond of you. What do we do about that?"

"Cake will freeze for months. Put it in the freezer until you decide."

"What about Mark?"

"I don't think you should freeze him. It's up to you though."

Just then we noticed somebody arguing with Mr. Raferty. Charly scrunched down in her seat, but Mark had already seen her.

"I want this thing stopped! He's kidnapped her!"

"I'm not stopping anything until their ride's up. They've got ten more rides coming, and that's what they're going to get."

Mark stormed away, walked to a pay phone, and made two phone calls.

"Charly, what did your note say?"

"I think it was, 'Am being taken for a ride. Will explain later.' Is that bad?"

"Not usually. But Mark thinks you've been kidnapped. He probably found the torn up Ferris wheel ticket and came here first."

Mark stormed back to the Ferris wheel and began arguing with Mr. Raferty.

On our way down, Charly started to explain. But Mark lunged for me, missed, didn't get away soon enough, and was struck on the shoulder by part of the frame. The blow threw him against Mr. Raferty. Raferty and Mark fell down and in the process broke off the speed control lever.

We started going very fast. I put my arms around Charly and held her close to me.

Raferty was knocked unconscious. Mark got up, looked around, grabbed a long pole, and crammed the pole into the gear mechanism. The pole jerked out of his hand, throwing him against the ground. Suddenly the pulley for the drive mechanism snapped, and the Ferris wheel slowed down and stopped.

A few minutes later the police arrived, apparently called by Mark from a pay phone earlier. A police ambulance took away Mark and Mr. Raferty, unconscious.

Then Charly's mother and dad arrived.

Charly stood up to yell that everything was okay, but the motion caused one of the other cars to break loose and fall to the ground.

That was when the police told us not to move around and to be quiet.

"Roberts, I want you to throw down the weapon you used against the Ferris wheel operator and this girl's boyfriend. I don't want you harming the girl."

"No, I don't ever want to do that," I said to Charly.

"Roberts, you've already got a charge of kidnapping against you. Don't make it worse. Throw down the weapon."

"Sam, you're not cooperating."

"I don't have a weapon."

"Let's see if I can help." She opened her bag, and we sifted through the stuff she carried in it. Finally we found a pair of scissors, which we tossed down. It seemed to please everybody.

In a few minutes a fire truck with a ladder pulled close to the Ferris wheel. "Miss, just reach slowly and grab hold. I'll have you down in no time," the fireman on the extended ladder told Charly.

"If I jumped, I'd be down in no time. Let's go very slowly. See you, Sam."

In a minute I was back down on the ground also. After Charly talked to the police and after we called the hospital and had Mr. Raferty and Mark explain things, they undid the handcuffs.

On our way to the hospital, Charly explained to her parents that she probably would get engaged, but not at the party the next day, and maybe not to Mark.

"But what about the cake?" her mother asked.

"Freeze it," Charly and I answered.

That's just what we did.

Onward
Christian Soldiers

Not everyone can go to BYU, at least not in his freshman year when he lives only 15 miles from another college, Mark thought as he made his way to a desk in the large amphitheater prior to his first class at State College.

He glanced at the 60 other strangers who had also elected to take Sociology 119. Many of them were also freshmen, opening their cellophane-wrapped notebooks for the first time.

He looked to see if he could recognize any members of the Church. As far as he could tell, he was the only Mormon on campus.

Two rows ahead of him was a girl who caught his attention. It was not her long hair flowing softly over her shoulders or her high cheek bones that caught his eye. She was reading a Bible.

The instructor, Dr. Guthrie, entered the classroom. He wore a turtleneck sweater and carried an old pipe that he carefully filled with tobacco as he waited for the bell to ring. He looked to be about 30 years old. Mark's adviser had told him that Dr. Guthrie was one of the most popular teachers on campus. He had won teaching awards for the past three years.

Dr. Guthrie began his lecture by telling the class that he was a little "hung over" from a party the night before, but that he'd try to muddle through. He opened with a joke.

Mark looked around at the others in the class. For the most part they were happy to find an instructor who was "human."

Dr. Guthrie talked for a few minutes about the course requirements, then switched to another joke that ended with a string of swear words.

The class roared its approval.

117

The girl in front of him raised her hand.

"Yes," Dr. Guthrie said.

She stood up, cradling her Bible in her arms. She stood with dignity and said calmly, "I'm a Christian, Dr. Guthrie, and I believe the Bible is the word of God. The Bible teaches that taking the Lord's name in vain is a sin."

Mark stared at this beautiful girl with no make-up who had the courage to face 60 people and declare her standards. At the same time he felt embarrassed for her, knowing the reaction of the rest of the class.

Dr. Guthrie studied her thoughtfully for a moment, trying to decide whether to humiliate her in front of the class or let it go.

"What's your name?"

"Sara Taylor."

"Okay, Sara. Thank you. I'll try and control my language."

Dr. Guthrie examined his notes for several seconds, and then, looking up with a sly grin, announced, "Sara has just wiped out half my lecture."

Loud laughter pulsed through the large amphitheater.

"I'll tell you what. I've got four jokes I won't be able to tell today, but if anybody wants to hear them," he said, with a mischievous grin, "come down after class and I'll whisper them to you."

"Just send her out in the hall when you want to tell a joke," someone suggested.

"I'm afraid she'd be in the hall all the time," Dr. Guthrie kidded.

He's the Pied Piper of State College, Mark thought.

After class, while the rest stayed to hear the jokes, Mark followed Sara out of the amphitheater into the hall.

"Sara?" he called after her.

"Yes?" she turned to face him.

"I agree with what you said about the Bible."

"Do you? I didn't hear you say anything in class." She turned and hurried away.

As Mark drove the 15 miles home that night, he rehearsed in his mind that first class, trying to picture himself standing up as she had done. Deep down, however, he knew he couldn't have done it.

As he drove, he remembered his disastrous first-grade school year in a small farm community, reliving the panic as he attempted to answer a teacher's question but stuttered so badly she finally turned to someone else for the answer. On the playground that year, other boys in the class had mimicked him day after day until finally he would not even go out for recess.

They had moved to a larger town after that year, and careful professional therapy had helped him overcome the problem, but the emotional scars were still there. He couldn't speak to large groups.

The next class started out with Dr. Guthrie being careful to control his speech. He was an excellent teacher, Mark had to admit, and only used the jokes as a diversion to keep everyone awake.

Halfway through the class, sensing students beginning to tire of sociology, he told a joke that would have made any truck driver blush. There was raucous laughter from a group of guys who sat on the last row.

Sara's hand shot up again.

Dr. Guthrie saw her and, with a grin, announced, "Oh, oh, I've been a bad boy. Yes, Sara."

Again she rose to her feet, and with a calm voice said, "The Bible teaches that adultery is a sin."

"That may be true, Sara, but I don't believe the Bible. I'm an agnostic, and any reference you make to the Bible is meaningless to me. I am more interested in what can be verified and proven. Please confine your statements to something having intellectual merit."

She sat down. I wonder if Dr. Guthrie ever loses, Mark thought.

After class, Mark stopped her in the hall.

"Can I buy you a donut and a glass of milk?"

"Why?"

"I want to talk with you."

They went to the student union cafeteria and found a table in the corner.

"Sara, I admire you for your courage."

For the first time, she seemed to relax, realizing that he wasn't going to argue with her.

"I know I don't do it very well, but I have to say something. I just can't let him walk over everything I cherish."

That she dunked her donut in her milk made her seem a little more human to Mark.

She continued. "Before class today a girl came over and said that she hoped I wasn't trying for a good grade in the class. I asked her if she had been quiet in class because of wanting a good grade, and she said, 'Sure, I'll believe whatever he wants me to believe for an A.' ''

"Oh," Mark said, feeling a little condemned by the story.

"Why didn't you say anything?" she asked as gently as she could.

He looked at her eyes, trying to decide if he could confide in her. She did not carry with her any arrogance.

"I'm afraid," he answered honestly.

"Anybody would be nervous; that's natural."

"No, it's more than that. When I was young, I had a speech problem. I overcame that, but the fear of being laughed at is still there."

"Exodus, chapter 4, verses 10, 11, 12," she answered with a grin.

"What's that?" he asked.

"Here, I'll write it down and you look it up later." She wrote the reference on a napkin and gave it to him. He put it in his wallet.

"Are you a Christian?" she asked.

"Yes," he said, wondering how much more he should tell her.

"Someday you're going to have to show it. Jesus will help you."

He wondered why this girl, who had only a fraction of the scriptural knowledge about the Savior that he had could be so much better at showing her love for Him.

"Will you help me?" he asked her.

"Yes, of course."

"Dr. Guthrie knows his business, but maybe we could be more effective if we could meet him in his own arena, you know, 'intellectual merit.' My Sunday School teacher is a trial lawyer. He knows how to present a case before a jury. I'm sure he'll help us. Will you come with me to my Sunday School?"

"What church is that? she asked.

"The Church of Jesus Christ of Latter-day Saints. The one we go to is 15 miles from here. I could pick you up at your dorm."

Sunday he picked her up at 7:30 in the morning so he could attend priesthood meeting. She attended a Sunday session of Relief Society.

After class he saw her coming out off the classroom. She was upset.

"What's wrong?" he asked.

"Take me back to the dorms or I'm walking."

"Why?"

"This is the Mormon church."

"Yes, that's another name."

"And you're a Mormon?"

"Yes."

"You've been deceived," she said, turning and walking quickly out of the building.

He ran after her. "Where are you going?" he asked.

"Back to the dorm." she stopped and accused him, "You're not a Christian."

"How can you say that? How could a church that is named after the Savior not be Christian?"

"What about the Book of Mormon?" she said. "That's your Bible, isn't it?"

She turned and ran from him. He ran after her. After half a block she slowed down to a fast walk. She wouldn't allow him to walk beside her, and so he maintained a ten-foot distance behind her.

A few blocks from the church, a family driving to church who knew Mark stopped and asked him if he needed any help. He asked them to tell his parents that he'd be late. Before they left, he asked if he could borrow a copy of the Book of Mormon. They willingly agreed.

He had to run to catch up with Sara. By this time they were outside the small town and were walking along a gravel road that eventually led to the highway back to the college.

"Sara, you can't walk 15 miles."

"Watch me."

"Sara, listen to me. I'm going to read you the flyleaf from the Book of Mormon." She sped up, but Mark stayed close enough so she could hear him: " '. . . to the convincing of the Jew and Gentile that Jesus is the Christ, the Eternal God, manifesting himself unto all nations. . .' "

"Do you have several wives?" she snapped.

"I don't even have one, and if all women are as unreasonable as you, I may keep it that way."

She kept on walking.

A few minutes later, he tried again. "Sara, I'm going to read from the Book of Mormon about the Savior. Did you know that he visited people in the New World after his resurrection?"

No answer.

Mark began reading aloud in chapter 11 of 3 Nephi. As he began, she again sped up, trying to get out of hearing range of his voice.

It was difficult to both read and watch where he was walking. He fell down once but quickly got up and continued.

After a few pages she slowed down.

He read aloud to her to the end of 3 Nephi. It took two hours.

Then, finally, she stopped and turned around. "What you've been reading, it's in the Book of Mormon?"

"Yes."

She began walking toward him. She passed him, standing there, and kept on going, now heading back to town.

"Where are you going?" he called after her.

"Back to The Church of Jesus Christ of Latter-day Saints."

"Sara?" he called after her.

"What?" she asked, not breaking stride.

"Can I walk beside you?"

She stopped and turned around. It was the first smile he had seen from her that morning.

By the time they reached town, the other ward was about to begin their sacrament meeting. He ushered her to the second row.

It was fast and testimony meeting, and it was one of those meetings that you hope will never end. At one point he looked over and saw tears streaming down Sara's face.

After the meeting they drove to the home of Brother Packard, who was a lawyer and Mark's Sunday School teacher. He agreed to help them debate the concepts presented by Dr. Guthrie. They stayed so long that they were invited for a light supper. While Sara helped Sister Packard in the kitchen, Mark called his parents to explain what had happened. He also called the elders to arrange a time for the missionary discussions for Sara.

During the next week Mark and Sara prepared to debate the opinions of Dr. Guthrie. They spent several hours a day in the library taking notes from reports that would sustain their position in regard to chastity, family life, and use of drugs. They used a shoe box to file their notes. On Thursday they met with Brother Packard who coached them.

Friday night Sara received her first discussion.

On Saturday morning Mark took her rock climbing in the mountains near the college. She had never climbed before, so he chose an easy route.

The air was crisp, and the leaves on the aspen trees along the canyon had begun to turn various shades of gold and yellow. They were both quiet as they made their way up a rock cliff, talking only when necessary, somehow trying to disturb as little as possible the beauty around them.

Finally they reached the top of the rimrock and sat down. He pulled two apples from his small pack. They munched on the apples slowly and watched the morning progress into day.

She looks her best out here, he thought to himself. On campus, if she were placed alongside a girl who uses make-up, Sara would look plain, but out here where simplicity is a mark of beauty, she looks good.

"Last night I woke up and started to cry," she said quietly.

"What for?"

"The problem I face is, what if your teachings are true?"

"They are."

"Mark, you can't be right. God would've told more people. How many Mormons are there?"

"Four million."

"And those four million are right, and everybody else is wrong?"

"The priesthood has been restored."

"I know that's what you believe."

"What's wrong?" he asked her. "What's really bothering you?"

"Okay, I'll tell you. My mother. All last night I worried about my mother. She's dead."

"I'm sorry."

"So am I," she said, fighting back the tears. While she waited to gain composure, she picked up a small gold leaf from the ground and examined it.

"My mother was a good person. Dad and Mom were always dedicated Christians. I never was. When I was 14, I rebelled against them. I did everything I could to hurt them. When I was 17, I ran away from home. I wound up in California, living with a group of other girls who had also left their homes. We were pretty wild.

"One day I went with some other girls to hear an evangelist speak. We went on a lark, but as he spoke, my heart softened and all the bitterness left me. I made a promise to dedicate my whole life to Jesus. As soon as I could scrape up the money, I took a bus home.

"All the way home on the bus, I thought how happy Mom and Dad would be to see me that I'd finally accepted Jesus as my Savior. When I arrived home, I found that my mother had died four weeks earlier. She never saw me as a Christian. We were never united as a family."

She let the leaf slip from her hand and fall to the ground. "What about my mother? Is she to be condemned for never hearing about Joseph Smith?"

He reached into his pack and pulled out his Bible and also his three-in-one combination.

"Do you have an answer?" she asked, surprised at seeing his broad smile.

"The most beautiful answer in the world," he said, turning to the Pearl of Great Price.

In the afternoon they found a path in the woods and followed it for miles. They talked about many things, both large and small, but once, during their walk, she turned and asked if they could talk about the Savior, and it was like two people getting together and sharing news about a cherished friend whom neither had seen for some time, each sharing memories of his experience with that friend. Sara told of His mission to bring salvation to the world, and of His love for even those who have sinned. Mark told of His appearance to Joseph Smith and other prophets, and that He was speaking to a prophet in our day.

As he said good-bye to her at the dorm, she said, "Mark, I must tell my father that I'm learning about Mormonism. I owe him that."

Sunday night she received the second missionary lesson.

Tuesday night he picked her up at the library at closing time, and they drove to a diner on the highway for a snack. She seemed very distant and tense as he drove.

When the waitress came to take their order, Sara said abruptly, "I'll take a cup of coffee."

After the waitress left, Mark asked, "Why? Why did you order coffee?"

"Why not? Do you think I'll be damned if I have one cup? Are you that close-minded?"

"You've never ordered coffee before," he argued.

"There's no reason I can't drink coffee. I'm not a Mormon, you know." Her voice was sharp, her face hard.

"You're drinking it just to spite me."

The waitress put down two rolls and her cup of coffee and his glass of milk. Sara eagerly took a sip.

"Would you like some?" she taunted.

"No."

"Why not? Afraid it will kill you?"

"Why are you acting this way?"

"My father received my letter today. He called me tonight after supper and read me some things about Mormonism from a book he'd found in the library. They are quite different from what you've been telling me."

"And you're going to believe him?"

"Why shouldn't I? He's my father."

"Will you at least finish reading the Book of Mormon and taking the missionary lessons?"

"No. I'm through."

"And so you're just going to believe what is in some anti-Mormon book without completely investigating our teachings?"

"I'm past the rebellious stage. Do you know what I put my father through when I ran away from home? I can't hurt him anymore. I love my father." She hastily got up. "Good-bye, Mark."

She hurried out of the diner. He threw down a dollar bill on the counter and ran after her.

"Where are you going?" he asked, running to catch up with her as she ran along the side of the road.

She stopped to confront him. "Leave me alone!" she yelled. "Go find someone else to convert!"

"Look, you say you love your father. Fine. I'd expect that of you. But do you love your mother?"

"She's dead."

"I believe she's waiting for you to accept the message of the Restoration. At least give me five minutes."

They turned and walked back toward his car. He drove her to the parking lot near her dorm and parked the car. During that time, he tried to decide what to say, praying in his mind for help.

"Sara, you know a lot about the Bible. I want to talk about something that is in the Bible. When Jesus was on the earth, he was not accepted by most people as the Messiah. One of the reasons was that he was from Galilee, but the scriptures testified that the Messiah would come from Bethlehem. Do you agree with me on that?''

"Yes, but he was born in Bethlehem.''

"I know. Hundreds of people rejected him because others, some of them influential and smart men, 'proved' that Jesus was not a true messenger. Any one of those people who rejected him could have asked Jesus about the apparent contradiction, and he would have told them that he had been born in Bethlehem.''

"I wouldn't want to have made that mistake,'' she said.

"Sara, don't reject our message just because someone says that we're wrong. Study it out. Finish reading the Book of Mormon. Finish the missionary lessons. Pray and ask God if it's true. That's all I'll ever ask. Will you do that much?''

She studied his face carefully for a moment, then shrugged her shoulders and replied, "Okay, I will do that.''

Just before she left him outside the dorm, she reached out and held his hands. "Mark, I think we had better quit seeing each other. I will do as you've asked, but I don't want to feel any pressure to accept your teachings because of my feelings for you. That wouldn't be honest.''

And so they quit seeing each other except in their sociology class. Mark asked the missionaries after every discussion about her progress. She was having a difficult time.

Sara continued to voice her opposition to some of Dr. Guthrie's views, but it was in her own way, and many in the class enjoyed seeing Dr. Guthrie systematically destroy her arguments.

Mark inherited the shoe box with references on recipe cards because Sara did not feel comfortable using them, but he had not yet spoken in class. The fear of being laughed at, as he had been when young, prevented him from speaking out. At night he would resolve that tomorrow would be different. He would practice in front of his mirror what he would say. But when morning came, he faltered.

Sara never did falter.

Another month rolled by. As Mark began his fast on Saturday, he decided to pray for help so that he could overcome his fear of speaking. He spent the afternoon in in bedroom praying for help.

Sunday morning, as he drove to priesthood meeting, he was stopped by the state police.

"Could I see your driver's license?'' the officer asked.

"Here it is," Mark said, pulling it out from his wallet. "Is something wrong?"

"Your back license plate is about to fall off. You better get it fixed before you lose it."

"Thanks. I'll take care of it right away."

After the policeman had left, Mark put his driver's license back into his wallet. He noticed a small piece of napkin tucked in with the other cards. He pulled it out. There was writing on it—Exodus, chapter 4, verses 10, 11, 12. He read the scripture while still parked alongside the road.

He saw Sara at church and went with her to the class taught by the missionaries. Near the end of the class, one of the elders asked what her reactions were about learning about the Church.

"It's very interesting," she said lightly. "I think everyone should learn about other beliefs."

Mark turned to her, "Is that all you can say?"

"What am I supposed to say? I told you my father doesn't want me to become a Mormon."

"Is the message true?" Mark asked. "That's the first question to answer."

"I love Jesus," she answered. "Isn't that enough?"

"How much do you love him? Enough to be baptized into his church? Enough to follow a prophet who receives revelation from Jesus?"

"Mark, when we're together, why is it that I always end up crying?"

"Sara," one of the missionaries gently asked, "will you pray and ask God if the Book of Mormon is true?"

She stared at the wall for several seconds. Finally she answered quietly, "I don't need to ask. It is true. I've known that for days."

"If you know that, will you be baptized?"

"Don't you understand? I love my father. All he's ever wanted from life is that I follow in his faith. He doesn't want me to be a Mormon. It would hurt him deeply, and I've already hurt him so much. How can I ask him to let me be baptized?"

Mark placed his hand on her shoulder. "Once you gave me an answer for one of my problems. You told me, 'Jesus will help you.' Sara, he'll help you too."

On Monday, Mark arrived late and didn't get to talk to Sara before class. Dr. Guthrie stated that they would discuss changes in the past ten years regarding dating and marriage. He quoted a number of surveys that showed a marked change in these areas.

"Have these changes been healthy?" he asked. "I think they have. The old religious philosophy of damnation for doing what is labeled sin is almost gone, and good riddance."

Sara objected. "I believe that kind of physical intimacy is reserved for marriage."

"And who reserved it only for marriage?" Dr. Guthrie asked, obviously baiting her.

"God," she answered.

"I see," he said with a smirk that was shared by many in the class. The group of guys on the back row began to boisterously sing "Onward Christian Soldiers." Dr. Guthrie smiled and asked them to stop.

"Sara, I'm afraid your opinion is fast leaving the contemporary scene. Does anyone else feel the way Sara does?"

Mark knew that he must finally defend his beliefs.

"I do," he said boldly, standing up to face Dr. Guthrie.

"Oh?" Dr. Guthrie asked, surprised at finding anyone else who would support Sara's position. "And are you going to quote the Bible too?"

"Dr. Guthrie, I can understand that two people may have an honest difference of opinion, but you have delighted in making Sara look bad. I felt the implication from you that anyone who believes in Christianity is foolish. And I have sat by and let you do it. I should have stood long ago to defend my beliefs, but I didn't. This is hard for me to do. Is there anyone else in here who has felt uncomfortable with the way Dr. Guthrie has treated Sara?"

A girl's hand went up. Then another. Slowly, soberly, others raised their hands until there were 15 hands in the air.

"Thank you," Mark continued. "You seem to take great sport in poking fun at the Bible. Have you ever read the Bible?"

"No. Not completely. I've got more important things to do."

"Is it fair then to say that you are not an authority on the Bible?"

Dr. Guthrie's smile had disappeared. "Yes."

"On what basis do you choose to reject a book you've never read?"

"That's beside the point. This is a sociology class."

"I'll get to that in a minute, but will you agree that there may be merit to the teachings of the Bible, but Bible study has been outside your area of expertise, and so we may treat your opinions on that subject differently than we might were you to speak about your area of research? Is that a fair statement?''

"Yes,'' Dr. Guthrie said grimly.

"Thank you. I'd like to make one small suggestion about your teaching. I can see why you are rated so highly as a teacher. You deserve the tribute you receive. However, I have noticed that you seldom present more than one side of any issue. That to me is not very scholarly.''

Mark wished he had time to write out what he was saying in order to filter it. He was making mistakes, angering Dr. Guthrie, but he had to muddle through as best he could. He felt the sweat pouring down his shirt, and he knew that he was blushing.

"Last week you chose to speak about the legalization of Marijuana. The week before we discussed open-coed dorms. In each of these issues your opinion matched that of the majority of the class. Today we will discuss a subject that, when we are through, will end up with you agreeing with the majority of the class that traditional religious sanctions on dating are old-fashioned. I am curious why you have chosen topics upon which you must know beforehand that there will be agreement between you and the class. Is that the price you pay for popularity as a teacher?''

There was utter silence in the room.

Too strong, Mark thought.

"Are you through?'' Dr. Guthrie asked curtly.

"I'm sorry if I've offended you. I don't want to change anything in the class except to add a more balanced approach to the topics we discuss. If you would not be offended, I am prepared to present tomorrow an opposing viewpoint to your position concerning the subject of dating standards.''

After class Sara met him in the hall. "I'm proud of you,'' she said. "Can we go for a walk?''

It was snowing lightly that morning. Large flakes settled gently on the lawn and trees and her hair.

"I called my dad this morning, and I told him that I loved him, and that I loved my mother—more now than ever before. I told him that Jesus has restored his gospel to the earth. I told him that this church holds the only opportunity that our family can ever have to be united together in heaven. I asked him to give me permission to be baptized. Mark, he said yes.''

He threw his arms around her, lifted her off her feet and they spun around and around until they both fell down on the snow, laughing, crying, bubbling.

In a few minutes they continued their walk.

"After I talked to my father, I phoned Sister Packard and asked her to help me fill out a form so that someone can be baptized for my mother in the temple."

"You've had a busy morning," he said.

"We've both had a busy morning," she said, squeezing his hand as they approached the cafeteria. "But you know what? It's just the beginning of busy mornings and afternoons for both of us."

"Why's that?" he asked.

"This morning, when I phoned the missionaries to tell them I wanted to be baptized, we also talked about something else. Who do we need to contact about setting up an LDS institute program on campus?"

You Can't Save Cotton Candy

The dust chased the racing engine of the small import as it labored up the canyon road. It nearly succeeded in enveloping the car at the turn-around curve of each switchback only to be left behind as the gears changed and the complaining engine sped up. Near the top of the ridge the car turned sharply to the right, coasted up a slight incline to a small level opening overlooking the valley below, and stopped. The dust caught up with its now silent prey.

They sat in silence and watched the valley begin its transformation from day to early evening. After a few minutes, he opened the window, sniffed the last remains of the settling dust, and then opened his door to get out. "Well, here we are at Lover's Leap. Ladies before gentlemen!" he said, as he opened the door for her.

They walked a short distance up the ridge to a large boulder. It was level enough near its base to serve as a chair for her as they attempted to find from this viewpoint the location of their homes among the orchards, fields, and tiny towns that made up their valley.

From that lookout the valley ran for fifteen miles to the north and twenty-five miles to the south. Its boundaries were fixed by the mountains that surrounded it on all sides.

"Brad, does it seem good to be home again?" she asked.

"You know, I think a large part of me is still back there giving discussions. It was, let me see, just twenty-six hours ago that I left my mission president and his wife at the airport. The plane flew home in about the time it took to figure out how to open the salad dressing lid on my supper. When the plane landed, I was in a different world. There was my mom and dad, brothers and sisters, my dog Smart, and you."

"Listed in the order of their importance?" she teased.

"No, of course not. I'd rate Smart above my brothers and sisters. But what I want to know is, where on that ride did I change from Elder Roberts, missionary, to Brad Roberts, college dropout? Should I have asked the stewardess to help me drop my former identity out of the plane?"

"No. I think that if you ask for anything unusual on a plane now, they just fly you to Cuba."

"This morning I woke up at six. I was racing for the shower to ace out my companion and just got to the door when I realized there was nobody to beat. I was home."

"So you decided to get back to a civilized way of life and went back to sleep?" she asked.

"No, I went fishing."

"And how did you do?"

"Don't ask."

"Brad Roberts, do you mean you were skunked?"

"Zero fish. It's the full moon."

She laughed. "That's what my dad says when he doesn't catch any fish—or else the river is too high or too low or under-stocked."

"My old fishing hole, the one I kept secret from my brothers, the one you have to walk down the railroad tracks for a half mile and then into a bunch of trees to get to—I went there this morning."

"By the way, how is it that you took me there once? Weren't you afraid I'd tell everybody?"

"You are so bad at giving directions I knew that anybody you'd tell would wind up somewhere in the middle of a corn field in Nebraska."

"Well!" she said, faking insult.

"So I tromp through the trees and what do I see across the river? A trailer camp with maybe a hundred campers and trailers. There's no fish there now. All those guys from California or Montana or some place have taken my fish and gone. You know, I used to get my limit in an hour all the time there."

"Has anything else changed, Brad?" The question, as she had intended it, should have evoked a discussion of the new motel, or the new stretch of interstate highway, or the addition to the ward chapel, or the way his brothers had grown in two years. But a certain edge in her voice betrayed her.

He caught the uncontrollable change in direction. "Whatever happened to Cathy Miller?"

"Isn't she still waiting for Brad Roberts to get back from his mission?" she replied.

"All this time? Good grief, she waited all this time?"

"The happiest two years of his life," she teased.

"What was it like for you?" he asked.

"The easiest thing in the world. I just called up all my old boyfriends and told them I was available."

"Really? I knew you went and joined the Peach Fuzz Festival just for publicity; you know, for those guys who may not have been blessed to have been born in our fair town but could still read the paper."

"It was the Strawberry Festival."

"Cathy, what was it really like?"

She thought a while before answering. "After you left, I imagined I could wrap my life in Saran Wrap and let it sit for two years until you came back. But it's a sterile existence to try to stop living and watch the clock tick. I couldn't do it, Brad. I've had a busy life since you've been gone. But I always had a little comfortable room in my mind where memories of you hung like pictures from the walls. I often visited that room and remembered how good it was when we were together. That's the way it was, Brad. You didn't want me to tell you that I cried myself to sleep every night, did you?"

"No, Cathy. I never wanted that."

They had walked back to the car. The sun had dropped down behind the mountain across the valley from them.

He reached through the window, opened the glove compartment, and pulled out a small package. "Cathy, I've got something that I want you to have."

She opened it up. An engagement ring lay mounted on a velvet cushion.

"It's beautiful, Brad." She spoke quietly, her voice nearly cracking.

"I bought it two years ago before I left." In case she might not realize, he added, "Cathy, it's an engagement ring."

"I know, Brad."

"Will you marry me?"

She touched his hand lightly. "Brad, could we sit down for this?"

The cold silence beat its fury on them as he helped her into the car and walked around to the driver's side and got in.

"Brad, why did you do this?"

"Because I want to marry you."

"Why do you want to marry me?"

"We've talked about this before, Cathy. We agreed we would get married if you were still here when I got back."

"And so now you feel obligated to me for waiting for you?"

His words leaped out. "Have you decided to go into law, for crying out loud! Why have we been writing all this time? Why did you go to summer school while I've been gone? So that you could work while I finished school. Why have you spent so much time with my parents while I've been gone?"

"You do feel obligated to me for the last two years, don't you?"

"You're twisting my words! You do remember that you said you would marry me, don't you?"

"That was two years ago, Brad! Maybe you can say that it seems like you just left yesterday, but I can't say that. It seems to me like you left ten years ago!"

He was confused and off balance. "I love you, Cathy," he said softly.

"Why, Brad, you don't even know me now; how could you love me?" Her words seemed to hit him. "Do you know who you love? You love a girl that doesn't even exist anymore—a girl with my name but two years younger than me. You go ask her to marry you. But she won't. Because she loves someone with your name but two years younger than you. You wouldn't stand a chance with that girl."

"What are you trying to tell me?"

"That I can't accept your ring. At least not now."

"Is there someone else?"

"Not really."

She touched his arm. "You don't owe me a thing, Brad. Most of all, you don't owe me a proposal of marriage as a payment for waiting for you. I am not going to hold that club over your head. When I kneel across the altar in the temple, I've got to be certain that it's the right guy for me and I want him to be convinced too."

She handed him the jewelry box containing the ring.

"Am I still in the running?" he asked quietly.

"You are if I am, Brad. But with no pressure because of what we've talked about or written in the past. And not because our parents wish it. And not because of what it was like two years ago. You can't save cotton candy."

"You can't what?"

"I was just remembering something that happened to me when I was a little girl. My father took me to a carnival and bought me some cotton candy. It was pink and looked like the clouds at sunset. I just thought it was the most beautiful thing I'd ever seen. When we got home, it was time for bed. I decided to save it so that every day I could have it and look at its beauty. I put it in a little box and put the cover on. The next morning when I woke up, I rushed to look at my beautiful treasure. There was just a lump of sugar and a sticky cardboard funnel. I cried because I thought someone had destroyed it. When I told my mother that I had wanted it to last forever, she said, 'You can't save cotton candy forever, you have to make a little every day.' "

They took a long silent look at their valley. The several small towns could be seen as small clusters of light around the darkness defining the lake.

"Cathy?"

"Yes?"

"Thanks. Is there anything else I should know?"

"Yes, Brad."

"What is it?"

"I'm hungry."

A hint of a smile swept across his face. "Well, at least that hasn't changed."

"Watch it, fella! That's no way to talk to Miss Strawberry Festival."

"Let's go to the taco place we went to before I left."

"We can't. They tore it down last year."

The car backed slowly down to the road, stopped, and then in low gear crept down the dusty road.

The Changing
of the Guard

The bishop asked me later if I knew when I visited the old man that Sunday afternoon. I guess I did.

"Jamie, come in. And you got Mark with you too. Come on in."

We stood in front of him as he lay in the hospital bed. "Mark, crank me up so I can get a good look at you both." Mark looked at him with a puzzled expression. "Down at the foot of the bed, you see a big handle there? Looks like they took it from a Model T, don't it?" Mark finally found it. "You turn that a few times and I'll be able to see something besides the ceiling." Mark turned the handle and the upper end of the bed began to rise. "Not too much. I don't want to be bent double. There, that's fine."

"Jamie, it's good to see you." He put out his hand for me to shake. I knew he was pretty sick because his grip was so weak.

"I got permission from the bishop for Mark and me to come and give you the sacrament."

"I'd be pleased to take it, boys."

We closed the door to the hall, and I took a small slice of my mom's homemade bread and put it on a paper plate. Mark filled a paper cup with water. I took the bread and carefully broke it and then knelt down and read the prayer. Afterwards I held the plate while he reached down and guided a piece to his mouth. Then Mark knelt down and blessed the water and handed him the cup. He spilled a little of it, but mostly he did fine. When he finished, he had tears in his eyes. "Thank you, boys."

Mark sat around for a few minutes and then said he had to go home. He didn't know the old man like I did.

The old man and I sat around and talked a little and watched the afternoon shadow move across the floor.

He was very old. His face was tough as if the wind and sun had carved out the soft flesh and left only the leathery surface. For 60 years he had farmed in the valley until his children had grown up and left, his wife had died, and he was alone with his garden, a plug horse named Blaze, and the Church.

I guess he'd always been in our ward, but kind of in the background. But I remember he used to bear his testimony nearly every month, and whenever Dad took me to the welfare farm for a work party, he would always be there.

When I turned 14 and was called to go home teaching, I was assigned to be his companion. He didn't have a car and I didn't drive then, so I rode my bike over to his place, now just a little way out of town since things had grown so much since he first moved there.

His living room had a round kitchen table with four chairs around it, with a shaggy throw rug on the floor and a reading lamp that hung from the high ceiling. Lying on the table was a large copy of the Book of Mormon and a Bible.

He shuffled over to the reading lamp and switched it on. Once he told me a horse had kicked him and left him with a limp. He stood there looking at me and then reached in his back pocket and pulled out a large handkerchief and wiped his nose.

"Jamie, we got to have a word of prayer." He grabbed the edge of the table for support and lowered himself to a kneeling position with his hands folded on the seat of the chair. Then he looked up at me and said, "You kneel, don't you?"

I knelt down.

"Father in heaven," he began, "Jamie and me come to ask thee to help us as we go as home teachers into the homes of thy Saints." It was a long prayer, and my knees were soon aching, so I tried to shift my weight around to get a better position, but by the time I found it, he had finished.

"Jamie, help me up."

I reached down and put my arm under his elbow and pulled. He was a big man, and it was a struggle to get him on his feet.

He walked over to the window and looked out.

"Come over here. Do you see the place over there by the big tree, and the place next to it down the road? On the way here, do you remember seeing the place with the 'Rhubarb for Sale' sign nailed to

the fence?" I *nodded my head. "The Lord's given us stewardship over those families. Do you know what that means?"*

"Yes sir."

"What does it mean?"

"Well we have to visit them once a month."

He rubbed one hand over his stubble beard. "Is that what you think it means?"

"I think so."

"You got a long way to go, son."

The nurse came in and gave him some pills. He didn't look very good. But when he talked, and you forgot about the chalky grayness of his face and his short, quick breaths, he was the same.

"Did you go fishing yesterday?"

"No, I'm waiting for you to get out so we can go together."

He looked out the window for a long time, and I thought he hadn't heard me. But after a few minutes he turned to me.

"Jamie, you better learn to tie your own flies. I can't furnish you with free equipment your whole life."

"I will."

"I would have taught you before, but you were such a slow learner at fishing. I thought I'd better wait."

The first time he offered to take me fishing behind his place, I brought the stuff my friends and I used when we fished from the old country bridge.

"What kind of a rig you call that?" He looked at my large lead sinker and a treble hook with a wad of dried-up cheese stuck to it. "Here, let me see that. You're not supposed to club the fish to death." He took the sinker from the line. "And whats this?" he said, pointing to the cheese. "You bring your lunch?"

"I usually use worms or cheese for bait."

He shook his head. "I'll teach you to fly fish. Then you'll know something about fishing."

He stepped a little ways into the river so he could get a free swing with his fly rod. "Look over there, just in front of the boulder." He whipped the fly line back and forth a couple of times to let out line, and then cast. The fly landed gently on the water and glided into the swirling water downstream from the boulder. Suddenly the water boiled as a German Brown rose up and took the fly. He carefully fought it to his side and then reached down and swished it up in his net. "You think you can learn to do that?" he said as he reached down into the net and pulled out the trout and dropped him gently back into the water.

Nearly every weekday afternoon that summer I'd go over to his place with my rod, and we'd walk across his field to the river. He taught me how to cast a fly rod, and where to stand, and what kind of flies to use for each part of the summer. "You got to find out what they're feeding on, Jamie. That's the secret."

He slept a while because of the pills. The bishop stopped by to see him, but saw him asleep, and said he'd come back later.

The second month that we went home teaching, Brother Johnson had just bought a new horse. And so we walked out to the corral and took a look.

"Mort, how much you pay for that mare?"

"About a thousand dollars. Why?"

"She's a fine horse. How come you spent so much money for her?"

"She's got a good line." Then he stopped and looked at the old man. "Why are you asking me a question like that? You been around horses most of your life."

"I never had a horse worth a thousand bucks. What will you do with her, sell her to the glue factory?"

"You know I'm not going to do that."

"Yep, I know that." He looked at the mare for a while and then turned to Brother Johnson and said, "Mort, how long did your dad serve as a bishop?"

"About ten years, I guess. Why?"

"You come from a good line, Mort. As far as the Lord is concerned, you're registered stock. But you're no good to the Lord the way you are now. It'd be less of a waste to sell the horse to the rendering plant as for you to keep away from church any longer. The Lord wants you back in harness, Mort."

Brother Johnson took the toothpick out of his mouth and dropped it on the ground. "You may be right," he said simply.

When the old man woke up, he was embarrassed that he'd fallen asleep. But I said it was okay; I didn't mind, and it would make him get better fast.

"Jamie, you been here too long. Your folks'll be worrying about you."

"It's okay. They know I'm here."

He turned his head so he could see outside. "What day is it?"

"June 13."

"June 13. Now starting in a few days, I'd try an Adams with a number 14 hook. You got enough flies? If you need any, you know where they are."

All of a sudden he seemed to get some strength, and he leaned forward. "Now, you keep visiting them families, you hear? The Johnsons are coming along fine, but you ask the bishop to get the Scoutmaster over there to get their boy Brad in Scouting." He grabbed my hand and squeezed it hard, and there was an urgency to his voice. "Jamie, you keep yourself clean so you can marry a pure and beautiful LDS girl in the temple when the time comes. And get ready to go on your mission. You need to read the scriptures more than you do."

"I will."

He still was holding onto my hand. "Jamie, once on my mission I went and saw the changing of the guards. . . .Jamie . . ."

Before he could finish, a nurse stuck her head in the room. "I'm sorry but visiting hours are over."

He released the grip. "You'd better go, Jamie. Come back tomorrow if you can."

The next day when I got home from my softball game, my mom told me he had died that afternoon.

I walked over to his place and down the path to the fishing spot on the river where we used to go, and sat down on a rock. The river takes a bend just upstream from that point, and there was a hole where the eddy currents curled around in slow lazy loops, and there, he told me, the fish stayed when they were feeding on a hatch of flies coming down the river. The spot was hard to find because of the growth of trees on both sides, and most people who fished it probably got their line tangled in the fallen branches that lay in the water. But he told me where to stand and how to cast so you avoided the hidden traps.

My thoughts were interrupted by a trout jumping clear of the water for a fly. And then, for a moment, I could hear in my mind the old man say, "Don't whip the water, just let it slide down nice and easy. You're supposed to make the fish think a fly is landing on the water and not that a tree has fallen into the water. Use the Royal Coachman now, Jamie. How come you've never read the Book of Mormon? I want you to read it, and in three months I want you to tell Brother Johnson about it and bear your testimony."

I sat there for a couple of hours thinking about him until finally it was too dark and I got up and walked back down the path to my home.